"DON'T YOU AIM TO STAY A SPELL AND PLEASURE US?"

"I'd be a liar if I denied that your offer tempted me," Longarm said to Rosemary. "But I'm on duty and I ain't sure a census taker's supposed to get so personal."

"Kill him if he tries to leave," suggested Lavender from the bed.

Longarm laughed. "Well, I would be a sissy if a lady had to pull a gun on me to get me to kiss her."

So he kissed her. Rosemary dropped her gun and flattened her thinly clad body against his, as her sister on the bed started crying out, "Oh, he's staying, and we're gonna have some fun!"

TABOR EVANS

LONGARM

IN DEADWOOD

A JOVE BOOK

LONGARM IN DEADWOOD

A Jove Book / published by arrangement with
the author

PRINTING HISTORY
Jove edition / June 1982

ISBN: 0-515-05601-4

Jove books are published by Jove Publications, Inc., 200 Madison
Avenue, New York, N. Y. 10016. The words "A JOVE BOOK" and
the "J" with sunburst are trademarks belonging to Jove Publications, Inc.

PRINTED IN THE UNITED STATES OF AMERICA

Chapter 1

"Oh, my God, it's my husband!" gasped the blonde in bed with Longarm. But Longarm didn't answer. He'd evacuated her fleshly delights and was rolling out of the four-poster by the time the infernal woman figured out who in tarnation was fumbling with the front door lock in the dark. No man with a lick of sense allows himself to be caught bare in the saddle when he has his pants and a double-action Colt .44 hung over the back of a nearby chair.

Longarm had made it to the chair and his possibles when a male voice in the next room called out, "Honey, I'm home!" So, seeing it wasn't a burglar, Longarm picked up chair and all and rolled out the open bedroom window on his naked rump to land crouched in the side yard, chair, duds, guns, and—Jesus, where were his boots?

The boots sailed out the window over his head as he sat in the dirt, hauling on his pants. He grinned sheepishly, but

1

didn't call out his thanks. He could see by the wavering square of light against the blank wall of the house next door that someone had come into the bedroom with a lamp, and sure enough, he heard the infernal blonde call out, "Why, Silas dear, you startled me. I thought you were the Big Bad Wolf, or worse. You're supposed to be in Salt Lake City!"

A male voice answered, right over Longarm's head, "Deal fell through and I caught the night train home to Denver. I'm glad I found you awake and naked, honeybunch. I'm randy as all get-out after being away from you so long!"

"Aw, shit," Longarm muttered as he quietly finished dressing in the shaded slot between the houses while just above him he heard the sounds of another man moving *his* duds in the opposite direction.

The blonde was likely aware they were being overheard as she protested, "For heaven's sake, Silas, I'm hardly awake yet! What time is it, anyway?"

"Must be nigh five in the morning, little darling, for I heard a cock crowing as I come along the walk out front. And speaking of cocks, I got me one here that's been crowing for you all the way from Salt Lake City!"

The light went out. But Longarm was almost finished, and he felt more comfortable pulling his boots on in the dark, for the two of them were making enough noise in there to wake the dead, and should a nosy neighbor see fit to peer out that upstairs window, Longarm would likely feel even dumber.

He had himself buttoned presentably by the time the unexpected husband was torturing the springs of the four-poster he'd just been enjoying the same way. So Longarm rolled on his hands and knees and started crawling off as he heard the gent laugh and observe, "I knowed you was hot as well as lonesome, honeybunch, for your gates of paradise are already gushing for joy!"

Longarm didn't hang around to hear her answer. He rose

with a grimace to stroll innocently out of the slot between the houses, and the tree-shaded street out front was deserted, praise the Lord. The sky was growing pearly and, sure enough, as he paused to light a cheroot a couple of houses down, he heard a backyard rooster announcing the pending arrival of the sunrise. Longarm muttered a fervent curse on all Monday mornings, and looked around for something to kick, but there was only the usual supply of road apples in the street, not very satisfying as kicking material.

Now that he was clear of that bedroom farce he hadn't rehearsed, it was time to study his options. It was too late to go home to his own furnished digs on the unfashionable side of Cherry Creek, and try for some shut-eye. But he sure needed some. The Junoesque blonde with the big blue bedroom eyes had told him she was a widow woman and he'd believed her; she'd surely acted like a gal who hadn't had any loving in a hell of a long time. But hell, by the time he got home and in bed, it would be almost time to get up and go to the office.

On the other hand, it was too early to head for the Federal Building. It would still be locked up at this infernal hour. Longarm swung west at the next corner and got over on Broadway, south of the Capitol grounds.

Sure enough, that old Mex who sold hot tamales from his pushcart was open for business. He sold Longarm a tamale wrapped in newspaper and a soggy paper cup of what he said was coffee. It tasted like iodine, but a man needed something wet to wash a tamale down, so what the hell.

Other folks in Denver seemed to be waking up as Longarm strolled toward the center of town, eating and drinking on the fly. A nearly empty horsedrawn streetcar passed one way as a dray, loaded with farm produce for the wholesale market near the railyards, went the other. The sky was the color of a linen sheet that needed changing, and he could make out colors in the dawn light now. The State House

3

lawn was supposed to be green. But of course, this late in the summer the grass was more a welcome-mat brown; grass didn't stay summer-green worth mention, this far west, unless you watered it every day, and folks out here on the High Plains had better things to do with such water as there was.

The shade trees along Broadway were still green, though. Cottonwoods were good at rustling their own water from deep in the adobe soil. A young gal was leaning against the bole of a corner cottonwood like she was holding the tree up with her back. As Longarm approached, she called out, "Howdy, cowboy. Are you game for some fun?"

Longarm grinned ruefully and answered, "Not hardly, ma'am." But then he saw how young she had to be and stopped, frowning down at her. The girl's face was painted up scandalously, but if she was over twelve, he was a poor judge of female flesh. She met his eyes brazenly as he threw away his tamale wrappings and asked her, "Does your mother know you're out, girl?"

The girl pouted and said, "Don't have no mother, cowboy. But I got something else you can hire by the hour, and I ain't as expensive as them old gals down to the Silver Dollar, neither. How about it, cowboy? Three ways for six bits?"

Longarm lit another smoke before he told her, "I ain't a cowboy and you sure are sassy for a kid your age. What you're doing here ain't a federal offense, so I can't arrest you. But somebody ought to wash your mouth out with naphtha soap. Where in tarnation did a little gal like you learn to talk so dirty?"

"I ain't talking dirty, I'm talking business. You want to screw or don't you?"

Longarm stared down at her in disbelief as he noted that she'd be sort of pretty with a cleaner face and maybe a couple more years of growing. "Honey," he said, "you'd best go home and grow some hair on it before you try to offer it to grown men."

4

She laughed bitterly and said, "Jesus Christ, I'm selling it at half-price and the fool wants hair on it!"

Longarm walked on, shaking his head in wonder. Denver was getting to be a hell of a wicked place of late. Between married gals who were dumb enough to drag a poor innocent youth into bed under their own husband's roof, and streetwalkers maybe eleven or twelve, it was just as well he had a steady job to keep him busy.

He was awake now. He knew that by quitting time he'd be too tuckered out to get in any more trouble. He wondered what old Marshal Vail would have him doing this morning. He hoped it wouldn't involve much legwork. It was still too early to check in at the office. It might be a good notion to drop by the public baths and maybe a barbershop before he reported to work. For a happily married man, old Billy Vail had a keen nose for womanly smells, and it was tedious to be called a sex maniac by one's boss.

Hearing the clicking of heels against pavement, he turned to see that the child whore had abandoned her tree to its fate, and was now trailing the tall deputy along the sandstone walk. He noticed she wore high heels like a full-grown woman as she fell in beside him and plucked at his sleeve. "Come on, honey," she pleaded. "Don't be bashful. I may be a mite young, but I can show you tricks a lot of older gals don't know."

"I'll bet you could, at that. But you'd best lay in wait for somebody who don't shave regular yet. Let go my duds, honey. This is getting silly."

"You've *got* to come with me!" she insisted, and this time Longarm detected the fear in her voice. He stopped. That was something to study on. The little gal wasn't only far too brazen for a kid her age, she was scared skinny about something. As he turned to face her, with a view back the way they'd come along the base of Capitol Hill, she licked her painted lips and said, "Look, you don't have to pay me no six bits. I'll give my all for a quarter. Are you game?"

He started to shake his head. Then he spotted what he

was looking for; a gent about his size and age was leaning against a tree on the State House grounds, trying to look innocent. But what in thunder would anybody be doing there at this ungodly hour of the morning?

Longarm looked gently down at the girl. "Does your pimp really whup you for failure to attract growed men at such odd times and places, sis?"

She looked away and answered, "I don't have no pimp. I'm an independent businesswoman. That's why I'm free to set my prices so reasonable. Don't you think I'm worth two bits, handsome?"

As a matter of fact, he did. Longarm didn't go for stuff that young himself, but he knew there were men who did, and that they paid extra, not less, for pretty little gals. Two bits was too little by a long shot. The going rate for fresh young gals in any parlor house was more like two bucks these days.

"Can I assume you have some particular alley in mind?" he asked her.

"You come with me," she said, "and I'll treat you right in my very own house. It's back that way, near the Evans Grammar School. Do we have us a deal?"

He looked around and saw that no grown men, save the one by the tree, were near enough to tell him he ought to be ashamed of himself, so he said, "I was wondering how to kill me an hour or so, and this is starting to get sort of interesting."

So she took his arm and started walking him back the way he'd just come. The man lurking over there by the cottonwood pretended not to notice as they passed him, but when they got to the old Mex selling hot tamales, Longarm sure felt sheepish about the look he got from the old gent.

The young gal said her name was Doreen and that her digs lay off the alley running behind the grammar school. Longarm knew where the school was. It was a big sandstone pile, and naturally it wouldn't be open for an hour or so.

6

He resisted the impulse to tell the kid she ought to be thinking about getting to school on time. He felt silly enough strolling arm in arm with an infernal six- or eighth-grader, and he knew she didn't go to the Evans school anyway. He'd been down the alley she had in mind. The buildings facing the other way off the alley had high board fences blocking their view of the alley, too. Longarm didn't look back as Doreen led him on. He knew that the rascal working with her wouldn't make his move until they got to the alley.

The school was only a spit and a holler from the State House grounds, so they didn't have far to walk, but despite his pure intentions, Longarm had a semi-erection by the time they got there. The child was doused in musky perfume that made her smell like a real woman, and a man with any natural curiosity would have wondered by then if she really did what she said she liked to do with her tiny painted mouth. He could see how weaker-willed gents could fall for their setup. He hadn't heard much talk about Denver gents being rolled in alleys on their way to work, but then, it wasn't the sort of thing most men would see fit to report to the law.

"We're almost there," Doreen said, as she steered him by one elbow into the narrow and still fairly dark alley. She said her place was near the far end, in the inky shadows of the big old schoolhouse. Longarm had certain advantages on the pretty little decoy as they entered the dark slot. He'd once had a gunfight along the back fences and trashbins in here, so he knew the lay of the land as well or better than they did. As they started to pass a certain gap in the fences, he swung her in between the nearly touching carriage-house backs and growled, "You just shut up and freeze, hear?"

"I don't want to screw in here!" she gasped. "I'll get my dress dirty!"

He cuffed her softly, and she sobbed, "Please don't hurt me." "I won't," he said, "if you don't breathe hard enough for a mouse to hear!"

Then he drew his .44 and turned away from her as his own keen ears picked up the gritty shushing of boot heels on gravel, walking cautiously and a mite confused.

Longarm waited until the man following them drew abreast of their slot before he stepped out into the alley with a pleasant smile and said, "Howdy, you son of a bitch." He swung the barrel of his heavy revolver down on the man's wrist to make him drop the length of pipe he'd been packing in his right hand. The man howled like a kicked dog as he grabbed his broken forearm with his free hand, so Longarm pistol-whipped him to his knees and growled, "Hush your face, boy! If I'd aimed to wake up the whole neighborhood, I'd have just shot you."

The injured man rocked back and forth on his knees, moaning, "Oh, my God, you've busted my arm! I'll kill you both for this!"

Seeing that the fool just wasn't paying attention, Longarm brought the .44 down on the top of his skull to put him on his face, unconscious as well as quiet, before he turned and said, "You'd best come out here and explain this, sis. Your friend there ain't in shape to edify me worth mention."

The frightened child cowered as far back in the slot as she was able. "Please don't hurt me!" she whimpered. "I didn't want to do it! He made me!"

"I had that part figured out already, girl. I don't hit little girls in any case. Come on, I won't hurt you. I may have forgot to mention it, but I'm the law. My name is Custis Long and I'm a deputy U.S. marshal."

"Lord a' mercy! Are you the one they calls Longarm?"

"I'm afraid I am. And I ain't got all morning, so front and center, you little sass."

Doreen came out gingerly, gasped as she saw the still form on the ground, and wrapped her tiny arms around Longarm's waist as she buried her face against his vest and started to bawl.

Longarm stood quietly, his gun dangling at his side,

while he waited for her to simmer down enough to talk. He said, "If I'm any good at painting pictures, that rascal at our feet has been using you to lure unwary gents within reach of his lead pipe. Who is he, Doreen? I hope he's not kin to you, for if he is, he ought to be ashamed in the first place, and you won't be seeing much of him in the second. Rolling randy rascals in an alley ain't exactly a federal offense, but as a peace officer I have some leeway in such matters, and he figures to be making little rocks out of big ones of the State of Colorado for the foreseeable future."

"Are you going to arrest me too?"

"I'm still studying on that. Let's start with who the bigger criminal might be. What's his name, and how come I find him playing with children?"

Doreen sniffed and replied, "He's called Ohio. He said he'd hit me some more if I asked too many questions. We met up a while back on the road. He, uh, taught me the facts of life in the boxcar we was sharing on the UP line. I was on my way to California to be a gold miner or something. But he said he knew easier ways to make money, here in Denver."

"He was wrong. What were you doing in a boxcar at such a tender age, girl? You run away from home?"

"I had to. My stepfather wanted to teach me the facts of life too. I didn't know it felt so good when I run off, of course."

Ohio groaned and tried to sit up. Longarm couldn't think of a thing he wanted to say to a child molester, so he kicked him in the face and put him back to sleep for a spell. The sudden motion freed him from the little gal, so he put his gun away as he sighed and said, "Well, we sure have us a mess to clean up here. It's almost time for the kids to start showing up at that school down the alley, too. I reckon the Denver P.D. will be happy to take Ohio off your hands, Doreen. But what am I to do with you?"

"Do you want to take me home and screw me? I really

like to screw, and if you don't arrest me I'll be your French gal too!"

Longarm shook his head soberly. "Not hardly. My landlady ain't quite that understanding. She's still sore at me about a Mex gal who helped me bust her bed one night, and I'm sure she'd draw the line at anybody she found playing with dolls in my digs."

"Please don't send me to prison, Longarm. I ain't old enough to go to prison!"

"That's what I just said, damn it. If you was just the usual runaway, I'd send you home and say no more about it. But from what you tell me about your stepfather, I wouldn't be doing you or your mama much of a favor if I throwed you from the frying pan into the fire. We'll study on what's to become of you after I turn this ornery hobo over to the local law."

He bent over to shake Ohio's shoulder. "Rise and shine, old son. It's almost sunup, and I fear there's a county road that's just waiting for your attention."

Ohio didn't answer. His eyes were open as Longarm rolled him over, too. It was almost broad daylight, and Ohio's face was sort of pale. Longarm felt the side of Ohio's neck and straightened up, muttering, "Hell, folks who chase other folks down alleyways ought to have thicker skulls."

Then he took Doreen by the arm and added, "Come on, sis. We got to find us a copper before the little kids on their way to school stumble over our trash."

"Oh, Lordy, is he dead?"

"That's about the size of it. Come on, there ought to be a patrolman down near Broadway."

"We have to run away and hide somewhere!" she gasped, trying to pull free.

But Longarm hung on. "Simmer down, sis. I'm trying to break you of such bad habits. Folks don't have to run when they're in the right. I want you to study on that some. But let me do the talking until I tell you to speak up, hear?"

10

She was crying now, like the lost child she was. So he stopped, swung her to face him, and said gently, "Doreen, listen sharp to what I'm saying. I'm on your side. Do you believe that?"

"If you say so. I'll do anything you want, as long as you don't hurt me."

"I ain't aiming to hurt you. You've been hurt enough. You ain't old enough to be running about unsupervised. If I let you go, you'll just wind up in the hands of another rascal like Ohio, or worse. You can see that, can't you?"

"I'm so scared," she sobbed, trying to move closer. He moved her back, still hanging on to her arm as he said, "You have a right to be scared. But we'll get you fixed up later. I see a blue uniform and a billy club headed our way. So stuff a sock in your pretty little mouth and don't make liars out of your elders, hear?"

Longarm hailed the copper with a wave, and the patrolman cut across the street to join them, calling out, "Morning, Longarm. Are you working as a truant officer these days?"

"Not hardly. Taking little Doreen here to meet some folks. But I have a killing to report to you if you've got the time, Bailey."

The patrolman's face sobered as he replied, "A killing, on my beat?" and Longarm said, "Yep. You'll find a dead hobo in the alley back of the school down that way. You might clean up some alley robberies on the blotter downtown at the same time. His handle was Ohio, and he was prone to sneak up on folks with a foot of lead pipe in his fist from time to time."

Bailey blinked in surprise and answered, "By gum, I have heard of some gents getting hit on the head of late. Funny thing, though, none of them seemed to see fit to follow up on the charges, even when we found 'em laid out and robbed."

"Some folks don't like to get involved, I reckon. Anyway, Ohio won't do it no more. Like I said, he's dead over

11

behind the Evans Grammar school."

"I'd best call for the meat wagon, then. Who kilt him and how come you know so much about his misdeeds, Longarm?"

Longarm smiled thinly and replied, "I killed him. Spotted him following me on my way to work, so I cut down the alley, and when he followed me in with that pipe, I sort of tussled with him, and between one thing and another—"

"Good Lord! He tried to roll *you*, Longarm? He must have been new in town."

"He was. He and I exchanged a few words as he was, ah, resisting arrest. You wouldn't want to take the paperwork off my hands, would you, Bailey? It does get tedious talking to reporters, and what the hell, I've already had my name in the *Post* a couple of times."

Longarm could see the young copper's eyes as he rose eagerly to the bait by asking, "Won't you want a share in the credit, Longarm?"

Longarm dismissed the suggestion with a wave of his hand. "He's all yours if you want to fill out the infernal papers for the coroner, Bailey. I've got a busy day ahead of me and, what the hell, it wasn't a federal case. It would read just as good in the *Post* if you was writ up as the arresting officer, wouldn't it, Bailey?"

"I'd have to say I finished him off with my billy, wouldn't I?"

"Sure, but what else could you have done, with him swinging a lead pipe at you, old son?"

So Bailey said he'd do it, and they parted amicably as Longarm walked the runaway along Broadway, looking for a cab for hire. As soon as they were alone, the juvenile tart told him, "You sure lie good. I'll bet if we went to bed together for a week, nobody would ever know!"

"I'd know, sis," he said, "and every morning when I shave, I have to look myself in the eye. So we'll say no more about it for now."

"For now, handsome? What if I was a big girl of fifteen or sixteen?"

"We'll talk about it then, Doreen. Right now I owe it to my fellow grown men to leave you someplace where you can't tempt weak-willed gents with those wicked little eyes."

Chapter 2

The orphanage said they'd board the runaway at least until she was old enough to pass for a grown woman, and that they'd teach her some trade more fitting than the one she'd learned from the late Ohio. Longarm had thought he was being slick when he asked to speak with the matron, Morgana Floyd; he knew Morgana to say howdy to, and she was a nice-looking brunette who filled her severe black uniform well. They'd met on a streetcar after it had crashed into a brewery wagon. She'd been a mite snooty at the time, but he'd put that down to a combination of shock and the aromatic suds that were dripping from both of them. He'd been meaning to get to know her better, but with one damned thing and another, he'd never had a decent reason to come calling at the orphanage until this morning.

Morgana was blushing beet red as they sat alone in her office. Longarm resisted the temptation to reach for a smoke as he smiled across at her and said, "Her tale was a mite shocking. I told her on the way over not to use dirty words, but as you can see, she needs some discipline."

Morgana looked away as she composed herself and replied, "I've heard stories like hers before. It's my job to care for abused and abandoned children. But she does have a . . . pungent way of putting things, doesn't she?"

"I reckon you cleaned her yarn up as you wrote it down, Miss Morgana. Ain't it funny how you can say the same thing in Greek or Latin and it don't sound as shocking?"

"It's shocking enough, no matter how you spell it," Morgana replied, adding, "Isn't there some way to arrest that disgusting stepfather she reported, Mr. Long?"

He shook his head. "I studied on it, coming over. It'd be her word against his, and likely her mama's, even if it wasn't out of state. You could send her back to them if Colorado ain't up to keeping her and, well, you may have noticed she seems willing now. So he likely wouldn't whup her for running away."

The young matron grimaced. "That's a disgusting suggestion. The poor child needs reforming, and I can only hope there's time. We can't hold her once she's eighteen, you know, and her character's already suffered so much damage."

Longarm nodded, getting to his feet. He didn't think Morgana wanted to hear that little Doreen didn't feel all that damaged. It was a shame, in a way, when one considered how infernally pure both the orphan and her prim young matron figured to stay for the next few years.

She got up too, to walk him out to the front entrance. He noticed that she was breathing sort of raggedly, probably embarrassed by all the dirty talk they'd just been listening to. As he tipped his hat to say goodbye to her, she took a deep breath and said, "There's a dance being held in the assembly hall for charity this Saturday night, Mr. Long."

"Do tell? You've likely got your escort picked out, right?"

"Not exactly. I'll be in charge of the refreshments, as a matter of fact. But if you're free, we might, ah, talk about your little Doreen or something."

He promised to drop by if he wasn't on duty over the weekend, and they parted wistfully. He was a mite ashamed of himself for lying to a lady, but it seemed impolite to state flat out that the last place on earth he ever intended to be on a Saturday night in Denver would be a charity shindig attended by the likes of her. Morgana was as pretty as a picture, and he could tell she sort of liked him, even if he made her nervous. But he'd learned long ago that while a single lifetime presented an almost unlimited abundance of women, a man had only so many hours to live.

The side trip to the orphanage had put Longarm clear across the Platte River from the Federal Building, and even though he caught a cab and paid extra to get there fast, he was more than an hour late when he walked into Billy Vail's office. He perched on the arm of the red leather chair across the desk from his pudgy boss as he said, "Before you chew me out, Billy, I was up and on my way to work afore cock-crow."

Vail frowned up at him from the papers spread across the green blotter between them and growled, "Spare me the details, damn it. You've never made it in on time on a Monday morn within living memory, and your excuses are tedious to listen to. Lucky for you, I have you booked aboard the noonday Burlington. So we'll say no more about it."

Longarm took out a smoke and lit up before he asked, "Where are you sending me this time, boss? The Burlington goes all over creation, once it's north of here."

"You're on your way to Deadwood, Dakota Territory. Take a gander at this and tell me if you can see why."

Longarm reached across the desk for the typewritten sheet of onionskin paper Vail held out to him, and settled back to scan it. It appeared to be a voting registration list, dated for the coming fall elections. That seemed reasonable

16

enough; folks in the territories got to vote in national elections just like anyone else. Then Longarm saw a name on the list that didn't seem reasonable at all. He nodded and said, "James Butler Hickok's going to have a time voting this fall, Billy. He gave that same Deadwood address before he was killed four or five years ago. Of course, I could be wrong about the address, and some other gent named Hickok could be living in Deadwood these days."

"Keep reading," said Vail. So Longarm did. Then he nodded and said, "I see what you mean. There could be two gents named Hickok in a town that small, but I see Cockeyed Jack McCall is signed up to vote too. Didn't they hang him here in Colorado for gunning Hickok, a spell back? I remember reading about it. McCall's lawyer said it was unconstitutional to hang him in the state of Colorado for murdering a man in the Dakotas, as I recall."

Vail nodded soberly. "Whether McCall was hanged unconstitutional or not, it's unconstitutional as hell for a hanged man to vote."

Longarm handed the flimsy paper back as he replied, "I can see that someone's voting tombstones, Billy. But how come Washington's saddled us with the fraud? We're the Federal Court of Colorado. Do we have jurisdiction in Dakota?"

"We do now. The Justice Department's not too pleased with the answers they've been getting from the local marshal's office. This particular list of mysterious voters is a dead issue, no pun intended, now that it's been drawn to Dakota's attention that some of the folks on it have been dead a spell. Washington's asked me and you to make sure the next list is more accurate."

"It's a mite early to be worried about the fall elections, Billy. Who do you want me to cuss out up there, and more important, how can we make certain they don't just make up new lists as soon as I'm gone?"

Vail leaned back to fold his pink hands across his ample gut as he said, "That's the slick part. I ain't sending you

17

to supervise the fall voting, Longarm. Washington's sending its own special agents out to do that, once we supply 'em with some facts and figures."

"All right," Longarm agreed. "I'll go up and tell the locals to stop registering dead folks. The marshall in Deadwood ain't going to like it, but as long as we outrank him—"

"Back off and let a man finish," Vail cut in. "For a man who seldom sees fit to get to work on time, you sure have a way of jumping the starting gun, old son. I ain't sending you to swap lies with the Deadwood law, federal or local. You're going there to ride shotgun on the U.S. Census."

Longarm shot his boss a puzzled frown, and Vail continued, "That's what I said. The Constitution says there's to be a census every ten years, and there ain't been one for ten years now, so there's a crew waiting for you up to Deadwood, and the whole bunch of you are to census hell out of Deadwood and the surrounding parts."

"I know what the U.S. Census is, Billy," Longarm said. "Some jasper come to my door a spell back and asked me all sorts of fool questions about myself. I thought it was over by now. They knocked on my door along about April or May, now that I study on it."

"They sent a census crew to Deadwood too, this spring. Nobody ever saw hide nor hair of them again. That's why you'll be going along with 'em, this time. There's never been a proper census of the Deadwood area. Deadwood wasn't there ten years ago when they held the last one."

Longarm thought for a moment, then said, "I'm starting to follow your drift. Ten years ago the only folks around Deadwood were Sioux, but it's filled up some since they struck gold back in '76. Tell me some more about them vanishing census takers, boss."

"There ain't much to tell. A crew went out this spring, figuring to be finished by now, like everyone else. Folks in the town of Deadwood remember them wandering about, asking the usual questions. But after a spell, nobody saw

18

any of 'em no more and figured they'd just finished and gone back East. But they never. They just dropped out of sight without a trace. So now you know as much about it as Washington does. The new crew they sent has orders not to stir from their hotel until you get there. Your orders are to make sure that whatever happened to the first crew don't happen to the second."

Longarm nodded and said, "I'll do my best, boss. Do you suspicion that the gents who registered them dead folks had anything to do with the vanishing census takers?"

"Don't know," Vail said flatly. "It could read more than one way. A political gang who votes tombstones might have gotten upset by dudes from back East wandering about asking questions about names and addresses. On the other hand, Deadwood ain't the most peaceable neck of the woods for anyone who's got money and boots worth stealing. The stage lines up that way get held up with monotonous regularity no matter who's aboard, and since the gold mines have started bottoming out, there's a mess of desperate gents in and about a pretty wicked town. I don't suppose you'd consider taking along a few other deputies to back your play this time, would you?"

"I work best alone, Billy."

"This ain't the usual one-man job, Longarm. Those census takers won't be working in one bunch for you to ride herd on. They're supposed to fan out across country as they ask their fool questions. How in thunder are you to keep from losing track of one or more?"

"I'll figure that out when I jaw with 'em. If I have to, I reckon I can deputize me some help from the good old boys I know in those parts."

"Jesus, like you deputized Curly Bill that afternoon in Tombstone? I had a hell of a time explaining all them bodies, Longarm. A couple of 'em turned out to be innocent bystanders."

"Hell, Billy, the other side was shooting too. Me and

19

Marshal Earp parted friendly after I explained that I needed sudden help from Curly Bill and them friendly Apache."

Vail rolled his eyes heavenward and said, "Bullshit. We both know why you don't want to take along some boys from this office, Longarm. I've warned you more than once about your notions of rough justice, and if I hear tell of you shooting anybody unconstitutional in Deadwood—"

"Have I ever reported anything illegal on my official write-offs?" the tall deputy cut in.

Billy laughed despite himself and said, "No, and I've been meaning to talk to you about some of the expense-account vouchers you've turned in, too. How come you booked two Pullman passages coming back from Arizona alone that time, Longarm?"

"I was escorting a material witness," Longarm said soberly.

Vail snorted in disgust and said, "I heard she had red hair, too. Get out of here afore I cloud up and rain all over you, you sassy bastard. But, for the record, I offered you some hands to back your play in Deadwood, and I'm ordering you officially not to swear in no more highway robbers as federal deputies. You've time to take a bath and change your shirt before your train leaves, too. Take my advice and do it."

Longarm rose, looking innocent, and Vail permitted himself a knowing smile as he nodded and said, "Didn't think I'd smell she-critter on you, did you? I'll just *bet* you was awake before cock-crow, you randy rascal!"

Longarm grinned sheepishly and went out, blowing furious clouds of tobacco smoke to keep from shocking Henry, the prissy young dude who played the typewriter in the front office, as he picked up his orders and travel vouchers.

As he went to bathe and pack up, Longarm hoped Morgana Floyd at the orphanage didn't have as keen a nose as Billy Vail had, or that she would have blamed the musky scent of human rut clinging to his hide on the runaway he'd herded their way.

20

After Longarm had left the office, Henry went back in, carrying more papers to plague the chief marshal with. He said, "We just got a follow-up on that train robbery near South Pass, sir. Frankly, I expected you to send Longarm after that gang. Bursting through the brush after desperadoes is more his style than the, ah, delicate matter in Deadwood, don't you agree?"

Vail frowned up and at him and growled, "No. If I'd wanted Longarm to chase train robbers, I'd have sent him to South Pass. Hell, any deputy I have on the payroll is good enough to chase train robbers. You're right about the case in Deadwood being delicate. It's downright spooky too. We seem to have us some rascals too clever for the average lawman out our way, and too tough for the prissy detective gents Washington sends out from the East. Our wayward Longarm ought to be just the right mixture for the case. He's smart enough to figure crooks out, and mean enough to curdle milk when he does."

Henry shrugged his sloping shoulders and said, "If you say so, sir. But the last diamond in the rough who tried to tame Deadwood was named Hickok, and he didn't do so well."

"Hell," Vail snorted, "Longarm's smarter than Hickok. Meaner too, if push comes to shove. I ain't sending him up to Deadwood to tame the infernal town. But if Deadwood knows what's good for her, she'll mind her manners whilst our boy's in town!"

Chapter 3

Longarm arrived at the Union Depot loaded for bear and clean enough to invite to a funeral. Deadwood lay farther off from Denver in civilization than it did in miles, so the possibles strapped to his battered McClellan saddle included more than the usual bedding, clean socks, and such. Prices were higher in such places, even when you could find a general store that stocked your favored brands, so the saddle roll was heavy as hell. Longarm packed it in from the street on his left shoulder, balancing it with the Winchester .44-40 and two canteens filled with Maryland rye in his right hand. As he strode into the station, he saw his boss standing under the railroad clock with a worried frown.

Longarm glanced up at the dial and saw that he'd arrived with time to spare. He nodded and said, "Howdy, Uncle Billy. I wasn't expecting you to put me on the choo-choo twain."

Vail snapped, "Mind your manners. I ain't here to make sure you board the northbound flyer. I figured you were attached enough to your job to manage that. The Census Bureau's saddled us with another chore. Did you bathe and change your duds like I told you to?"

"Changed everything but my boots, hat, and gun rig. I even washed under my arms. Have a sniff?"

Vail scowled and warned him, "I said to watch that infernal mouth! You see that gal over there on the bench, under the big hat?"

Old Billy had understated her hat. It was a real pisser. The purple crown was decorated with white egret plumes. Then they'd wrapped the whole thing in yards of pale violet mesh to form a hatband and veil. The veil didn't hide the pretty features of the gal, and her matching purple dress was tight enough across the bodice to inform the public that either she'd been born with an eighteen-inch waist or she sure liked her corset tight.

A couple of heavy-looking carpet bags stood on the cement floor near the hem of her Dolly Varden skirt. She looked like she was loaded for bear too. But her traveling outfit was ridiculous if she was headed anywhere important on a coal-burning train. Vail told Longarm, "She's on her way up to Deadwood too. Census Bureau sent her over to us just now. I said you'd see she gets to Deadwood safely. So before I introduce you to her, I'm giving you a direct order to deliver her pure and fully dressed."

"Billy, that don't make sense."

"Sure it does, old son. All you have to do is keep your infernal hands out from under her skirts."

Longarm shook his head stubbornly and insisted, "I can stay celibate at least as far as Deadwood. But what in the hell's wrong with the Census Bureau? Can't they tell the he-males from the she-males like the rest of us?"

Vail shrugged. "They say she knows her business. I've met gals with enough sense to ask questions and write the answers down on paper, Longarm."

"Damn it, I ain't worried about her qualifications as a census taker. I'm worried about needless complications. And if you can't see that riding herd on a pretty female in rough country, where somebody's already been objecting serious to any census taking at all, could be a chore—"

But the brunette was looking their way with an expectant smile now, so Vail took Longarm by the elbow and led him over to introduce them. The lady census taker's handle was Charity Kirby. Longarm said he was proud to meet her. Then he put down his gear, shot another glance at the station clock, and said, "I sure hope you've got some less spectacular traveling duds, Miss Charity. We face a good four hundred miles if we had a crow to ride. Getting there by public transportation is a mite more complicated."

She smiled up at him and replied, "My railroad timetable says it's only a ten- or twelve-hour trip, Deputy Long."

He grimaced and said, "They ought to be ashamed of themselves for telling such fibs, ma'am. We have to change trains twice betwixt here and Deadwood, with the last leg by stagecoach. Don't you have one of them travel dusters like most gals wear to keep their serious duds presentable?"

Charity shook her head, setting the egret feathers waving, as she said, "I'm afraid not. Is there time to pick one up before our train leaves?"

Billy Vail glanced nervously up at the clock and said, "I fear it's too late, folks. I'd best get the two of you aboard. Try to find her a seat on the downwind side, Longarm."

Vail picked up the girl's bags. So Longarm sighed and followed with his own gear. A porter met them on the platform, and when Vail asked if the coaches hissing out there were the northbound flyer, the porter said yes and asked if they wanted their baggage with them or up front. Longarm said they'd be getting off just up the line at Casper, so by general agreement, he and the brunette wound up sharing a seat, with all their baggage on the one facing them. The porter said the train was fixing to pull out any minute, so Vail tipped him and left before Longarm could ask him half the questions he wanted to.

He settled for asking Miss Charity whether it was all right if he smoked, and she said she didn't mind. He'd just lit a cheroot when the train started up with a jerk, throwing her skirted thigh against his. She laughed and said, "I see we're on our way."

He wasn't sure how to take that. His boss had told him not to get forward with the gal. But he noticed she wasn't in any hurry to move away from him, even though there was plenty of room on the plush seat, and the trip was hardly started.

She asked him why they had to get off at Casper. He explained that they had to change to the eastbound Burlington there, adding, "We'll find out when we get to Newcastle, Wyoming, if the stage is still running from there to Deadwood."

"My timetable says we can get to Deadwood by rail from, ah, somewhere."

He blew a smoke ring and said, "Edgemont, Dakota Territory. We may have to ride that far if the stage ain't running the shorter way from Newcastle. Hairpinning back from Edgemont chews up a mess of extra miles."

She frowned, gazing out the window as the train picked up speed on the open prairie north of the Denver yards. "Isn't it six of one and half a dozen of the other, Deputy Long? It seems to me the trains are so much faster than any stagecoach that—"

"Call me Custis," he cut in, adding, "I know that either way we figure to arrive somewhere betwixt midnight and too-late-to-mention. But there's another reason for us to slip in the back way, by stage. The folks you work for must have mentioned the trouble they've been having up Deadwood way, and—"

"Trouble?" She frowned, turning back to face him in a way that put her knee tighter against his as she asked, "What trouble are you talking about?"

He rolled his eyes heavenward, then said, "Let me get this fixed in my head, Miss Charity. You just finished some census chores back there in Denver, right?"

"Yes, I've been doing office work all summer, and frankly it's an awful bore. So I applied for field work for a change of pace, and they said there were still openings in Deadwood, so—"

"So somebody at your bureau ought to be tarred and feathered for stupidity beyond the bounds of political patronage!" he cut in, reaching in his inside coat pocket for his notebook and taking a pencil stub from his shirt pocket. "You'd best give me some names to write down, Miss Charity. Who was the infernal idiot that sent you from the Denver office?"

She stared up at him in confusion. Then she said, "It was Mr. Doyle, I think he said his name was. I don't know his first name. You see, I signed up as temporary help and—"

"Doyle's good enough. Can't be more than one maniac named Doyle working out of the Denver office. I'll have Billy Vail check it out later."

As he put the notebook away, Charity asked, "Would you please tell me what on earth is going on? What are we supposed to be accusing poor Mr. Doyle of?"

"Probably just ignorant disregard for human life. But now that I study on it, almost *all* of you folks with the census get hired temporary every ten years. Be sort of interesting to find out if the idiot who assigned you to Deadwood works for Uncle Sam regular, or just comes out from under a wet rock now and again."

She moved away from him to sit up more primly, and her voice cooled off about ten degrees as she asked, "Oh? Are you suggesting the Denver office made some dreadful mistake in sending a mere woman out to take the census?"

He grinned at her and said, "Your qualifications as a census taker ain't at issue, Miss Charity. I'll say right out that I admire brains, no matter how they're packaged, and if they ever put it to a vote, I'm for women having the same say as anyone else in elections and such. Lord knows, no man who voted for Grant and Colfax has any call to consider himself any smarter than anybody human."

"Then why on earth are you so set against girl census takers?"

Before Longarm could answer, a burly gent with a day's growth of beard and the pungent aroma of a trailhand who hadn't changed his shirt or socks in living memory came down the aisle, stopped near them, and growled, "Your stuff's all over that seat I want, amigo."

Longarm glanced at the baggage on the seat across from them, nodded, and said, "There's at least a dozen other seats to choose from, friend."

"I don't want to sit nowhere else. I want to sit down here, where I can admire the pretty lady."

So Longarm shot him.

Charity screamed as the .44 in Longarm's fist roared while the bully was still going for the Patterson strapped to his right thigh. Longarm's muzzle flash set the surprised gunslick's shirt on fire as it filled his chest with lead and punched him backwards to sprawl in the aisle between the rows of seats.

Longarm snapped, "Stay down!" as he rose, his smoking .44 in hand.

He eyed the other startled train riders thoughtfully. They were looking at him like kids staring over a graveyard fence at midnight. The man who'd picked a fight with him had apparently been playing a lone hand, which seemed pretty dumb, when one thought about it.

Longarm called out, "It's all right, folks. I'm the law," as he moved forward to snuff out the smoldering flannel of the dead man's shirt with his booted right foot while he lowered the muzzle of his Colt, polite but ready.

The door at the far end of the coach opened, and a man wearing a conductor's cap and packing a drawn S&W came in. Before anything silly could happen, Longarm called out, "It was my gunshots you just heard, and I'm a deputy U.S. marshal. So come down here and help me sort out what happened."

The man recognized Longarm from other trips, so he nodded and holstered his sixgun as he gingerly made his way to where the corpse lay between them on the gently rocking deck. The conductor whistled under his breath and said, "You surely stopped his clock, Longarm. Who was he?"

"I was hoping you could tell me. I never saw him before. He just come up to us and started a fight over the seating arrangement."

The conductor looked around with a frown and said, "There's plenty of empty seats back here."

"I noticed. Noticed he had a waxed tie-down holster and a gun hand primed for sudden movement, too. That's why I didn't waste time on the usual preliminaries."

He glanced down at the corpse to add wearily, "I never have figured out why some of 'em like to build up a head of steam by talking ugly ahead of time. The more I study on it, the more it seems to me he boarded this train with my demise in mind. When do we arrive in Derby Crossing?"

"We'll be passing through directly. But the flyer don't make such local stops, Longarm."

"You'd best signal the engine crew about the exception, then. Aside from unloading this cadaver, I aim to send a few wires about his description and such. Meanwhile, you'd best send the porters back here with a sheet or something to package him neater."

The conductor hesitated, then decided not to argue, and said he'd see to his assigned chores. As he left, Longarm reloaded and holstered his Colt, and sat back down beside the ashen-faced Charity Kirby.

"As I was trying to explain when we were so rudely interrupted . . . " he began.

"You—you killed that man!" she cut in, staring at him like she'd just seen a ghost.

"Had to," he said. "He was either a maniac or somebody they sent aboard to make sure we didn't get to Deadwood. You see, somebody up Deadwood way doesn't cotton much to a federal census. That's why I was giving you a hard time about going there in a dress. Didn't they tell you in the Denver office that there's been some spooky nonsense in Deadwood?"

She shuddered and replied, "Of course not! I came out here for adventure, not to see people getting killed!"

"Well," he said, "we'll just put you on the train back from Derby Crossing and say no more about it. I doubt they'll fire you if you say it was my notion that Deadwood was a mite rich for your blood."

Before she could answer, the conductor came back with two baggage hands and a canvas tarp. As they spread it on the deck next to the body, Longarm knelt and said, "Hold on, boys. Let's see if this gent has anything to say for himself before we wrap him up."

The tall deputy patted down the man he'd just shot as the conductor said, "We're almost into Derby Junction, Longarm. I sure hope you ain't planning no other unscheduled stops."

Longarm tucked the dead gunslinger's wallet in his own side pocket to look at later as he stood up, saying, "I hope so too. Do you have any empty compartments in the Pullman car up ahead?"

"Sure we do. Hardly anybody books a sleeping compartment on this run. We figure to be in Casper afore sunset, if you passengers just let us run on time."

Longarm nodded and said, "Riding peaceable was what

29

I had in mind. You'd best book me a compartment whilst I unload this trash at Derby Crossing for you. You would have made an unscheduled stop in any case, had things gone the other way. I doubt this rascal figured to ride all the way to Wyoming after gunning a federal agent, so he'd have pulled the emergency cord. We just passed some riders leading a spare saddle bronc back yonder. Somehow I suspicion they might have been expecting to meet somebody out here on the lone prairie."

He felt the train slowing down and turned back to Charity Kirby, saying, "We're almost there, ma'am. I'll be proud to help you off with your bags if these gents here will carry the rest of what's unloading hereabouts."

She was sitting stiff-spined, looking out the window as though he didn't exist. She didn't turn her face to him as she said, "You killed that man in cold blood! He never had a chance!"

Longarm said, "Sure he had a chance, Miss Charity. All the fool had to do was stay away from us. I can see you don't like surprises, and I'm pure sorry if the noise offended your delicate ears. But if you'd been paying as much attention to him as I was, you'd have noticed he was slapping leather when I drew on him."

She just shuddered, as though she'd seen a snake out there on the prairie. So Longarm turned away with a defeated little smile. He saw that they had his present wrapped for the Derby Crossing law, and the train was going even slower now. Longarm led the way to the end of the car as, behind him, somebody whispered, "They say he's called Longarm. That gent who threw his life to the winds just now couldn't have been from Colorado."

He didn't want to delay the flyer longer than necessary, so as they pulled into the station at Derby Crossing, he swung down to land running along the planking of the small trackside station. There wasn't much else at Derby Crossing, not even a Western Union office. He jogged over to the telegraph shed the railroad used, and told the man at the key that he aimed to send some wires and that he'd pick up the answers in Casper. The telegrapher didn't argue once he spied Longarm's federal badge, so by the time the train crew had the corpse off the train and aboard a luggage cart, Longarm had scribbled what he wanted sent and handed it over to be tapped out at a more leisurely pace.

Some townies had been attracted by the unusual sight of the flyer sitting in the station at their one-horse flag stop. One of them was wearing a copper star, so Longarm introduced himself and explained what had happened as the conductor stood by, fidgeting nervously and staring at his watch a lot. The Derby Crossing constable said he'd deliver the body to the county coroner and keep an eye out for that bunch leading the spare horse. So Longarm smiled at the conductor and asked, "What are you waiting for? Don't you aim to make it to Casper by sundown?"

"I heard you moved fast, and I see I heard right," the conductor said. "I sent the porter forward to unlock compartment B. Told him to move your saddle and all into it, too. So if you'll just get back aboard we can be on our way."

Longarm beat him to the steps, looking down along the platform to see if anyone had helped the suddenly frosty brunette off with her things. He didn't see Charity anywhere, so he figured she was still aboard. He shrugged and turned right at the top of the steps to head for the forward Pullman cars. Billy Vail had told him to keep an eye on her. But if she didn't want to be neighborly, there wasn't anything he could do about it. He figured she'd get her confusion sorted out in time to get off at Casper, and once she did, it wasn't his problem.

He had to make his way through two more coach sections before he came to the Pullman cars, up near the dining car. By then the train was moving again, and when he glanced back he saw that the conductor hadn't followed him. Longarm figured he'd recognize the letter B when he saw it. He'd work out later which porter got the tip for moving his possibles. He came to the door of the compartment he'd hired, and tried the latch. It was open, just as they'd said. The tiny room was furnished with bunk beds on one side and a sink and commode on the other. The bottom bunk hadn't been made up for sleeping. It was just as well. Charity Kirby was seated on the green plush, looking like butter wouldn't melt in her mouth.

He noticed she'd taken off the foolish hat and veil, so he hung his hat next to hers as he said, "Howdy. I thought you was to get off back there, ma'am."

She licked her lips and said, "I have a job to do. I guess I have an apology to make, too. You see, I've never seen a gunfight before, and—"

"Hold on, little lady," he interrupted her. "I told you I could see you were upset. I'd like to be able to say I never saw a gunfight before, but they go with this job. They ain't pretty sights, so let's say no more about it."

"I have to," she insisted, licking her lips again as she shuddered and said, "That could have been you on the floor back there, and when I think of how mean-mouthed I was to you, I could just die!"

He took off his frock coat and gunbelt before he sat down beside her and said, "I wouldn't want you to die on my account, Miss Charity. But if I'm forgiven for making so much noise, it's time we considered the source. That gent I just had it out with was laying for us. *Us.* Somebody up Deadwood way has it in for census takers."

"My God, surely you don't think he intended to shoot *me,* too?"

"I don't know, we didn't have a long conversation. But he had five rounds in that hogleg, and you were sitting right next to me."

He took out the dead man's wallet, brushing his knee against hers some more as he moved his hip to do it. He opened the wallet as he explained, "His face didn't mean much, but I'm tolerable good at names, if there's any wanted papers out on the rascal."

He opened the wallet. It contained nineteen dollars in silver certificates, enough to guarantee the jasper immunity from a vagrancy arrest, but there wasn't even a business card or a laundry ticket to say who he might have been.

Longarm shrugged, pocketed the money, and tossed the empty wallet aside, muttering, "He must have considered himself a private person. The law back in Derby Crossing said he'd wire me in Casper if they identified the body."

Then he looked her in the eye and said, "I want you to get off at Casper. I have an hour's layover betwixt trains, so I'll be able to buy you supper and see you safely onto a Denver-bound train before we have to part company."

The little brunette's face was even prettier without the veil. But her jaw was set as she insisted, "I'm going all the way with you."

He didn't think she meant that the way it sounded, so he answered, "You could go as far as you liked with me, if I was going anywhere but Deadwood. Haven't you been listening to me, ma'am? There's somebody in Deadwood who kills census takers, which is what you are, no offense. That disturbance back there that upset you so could be just the greetings at the door. The real party figures to start when I get to Deadwood. And I *do* mean *I*, not *we*. You'll be getting off at Casper and I'll be going the rest of the way lonesome."

"But—"

"But me no buts, ma'am. Like the Indians say, I have spoken. They've already killed or kidnapped a mess of census takers in and about Deadwood, and there's no way in hell I'll ride in with a female target at my side. I'll have enough on my plate just looking out for my own self!"

"But you have your orders from Marshal Vail, Custis."

"Billy Vail gave me those orders before anybody tried

to gun you, me, or both of us. He told me to look out for you. That's what I mean to do. You can write a letter to your congressman when you get back to Denver. But Denver's where you're going."

He leaned back, having settled the matter in his own mind, as they rode a spell in silence, save for the clicking of the wheels under them. Then she asked, "What can you do if I refuse to obey you? Send me to bed without any supper?"

He frowned and didn't answer. He'd been afraid she'd ask a fool question like that. Longarm didn't enjoy giving orders any more than he liked to take them. But when push came to shove, he could generally get most men to do what he wanted without having to shoot or even pistol-whip them.

Getting a stubborn woman to do as he said was a harder chore. The Lord had endowed most gals with a natural resistance to suggestions from men—which was likely for their own protection, when one considered the kinds of suggestions they heard from lots of men. But damn it, he wasn't out to lead her down the primrose path; he was trying to keep her from getting hurt.

She seemed to enjoy the corner she'd painted him into; she laughed some more and said, "I suppose if I was very naughty, you could turn me over your knee and spank me."

He didn't answer. The idea was titillating, and this infernal train wouldn't be arriving at Casper for a good five hours yet.

She saw that she hadn't gotten a rise out of him, so she turned to stare out the window at the passing scenery, which was pretty dull, unless you liked to look at a lot of dead grass. The tracks ran north on the prairie apron of the Rockies, to the west. You could see the long, jagged crest of the range as a darker shade of slate blue on the far horizon. But that wasn't very interesting either, so he studied *her*. She had a nice profile, starting at the cinched waist and moving up to the dark curls piled atop her head. Her face was partly turned from him, but he could see how stubborn that jawline was built. He knew that if he just lit out on her in Casper, she'd follow on her own, and then where would they be?

Vail hadn't been thinking ahead when he'd told the Census Bureau he'd have a deputy escort the latest and likely most attractive census taker up to Deadwood. Longarm still hadn't figured out how he'd ride herd on the less attractive ones when he got there....

There was an outside chance that the gunslick who'd started up with him just now had been sore at him for some other reason, but Longarm doubted it. He'd made a mess of enemies in the six or eight years he'd ridden for the Justice Department, and more than one old boy he'd tangled with had made vengeful remarks as he was leaving for the graveyard or prison. But the timing was a mite tight for the would-be assassin to have been after him about some left-over threats. The last couple of owlhoots Longarm had put in the box had been too ornery to have anyone that fond of them, and in any case he'd been available for revenge on the streets of Denver for days and a couple of Saturday nights. Anybody knew it was safer to gun a man on Larimer Street in the dark than aboard a moving train in broad daylight.

He nodded grimly to himself, wishing he could smoke but aware that it wasn't possible unless he cracked open a window to let a little air and a lot of locomotive soot into the tiny compartment. As if she'd read his mind, Charity Kirby sniffed and said, "My, it certainly is getting stuffy in here."

He grunted and said, "Yes'm. That's likely why these compartments was available for hire. The companionway runs up the shady side of the train, and these bitty roomlets face the afteroon sun."

"Do you suppose we could have the window open, Custis?" she asked.

He shook his head. "I'm likely strong enough to crack

35

the window up, despite the way it's been painted shut. But I did that once on this run. There ain't any breeze out there, if I'm any judge of grass stems on a summer day, so we're running through our own smoke plume. If you look close, you can see the fly ash falling fearsome out there."

She took the railroad timetable from her lap and began to fan herself as she sighed, "I think I'd rather arrive a little soiled than suffocated. Won't it be getting even hotter in here as the sun moves more to the west?"

"That's why they put those window shades in up above you, Miss Charity. You want me to pull 'em down?"

She said anything might help, so he stood up and, after a little cussing under his breath, managed to free the stiff canvas shades and pull them down, plunging them into semidarkness. He offered to light the oil lamp on the bulkhead, but she gasped, "Lord, no! It's already too hot in here."

So he sat back down and they rode side by side in the warm gloom for a spell before she giggled and said, "My, this is a thrilling way to pass the time. You say we're still five hours from Casper?"

"Give or take forty-five minutes," he replied, explaining, "We make one express stop at Cheyenne. They'll be transferring mail as well as passengers from the Transcontinental there. Sometimes it goes fast, and other times it can be a bothersome delay. Either way, we'll likely get to Casper just before or a little after sundown. This old flyer gets up to forty miles an hour on the straight stretches."

"Well, I suppose we could play cards, if we had any cards, and if we could see what we were doing. Did you bring any cards with you, Custis?"

He hadn't. Longarm didn't enjoy playing solitaire, and most folks he met who wanted to play a little stud already had a deck of cards. He loosened the foolish shoestring tie the Justice Department made him wear on duty, and cracked open the collar of his hickory shirt. It hardly helped. But

Charity followed his lead by unbuttoning the collar of her purple bodice to fan her exposed upper chest furiously. "It's no use," she said. "I feel like I'm sitting in a steambath with all my clothes on! We have to have some air in here. Can't you open the window just a crack?"

"I can try. But you're going to get soot all over that fancy dress."

She nodded thoughtfully and mused aloud, "I suppose if I took if off and hung it inside-out in the corner, it would be all right."

"I beg your pardon, ma'am?"

"Oh, the lining's smooth silk, and any fly ash that reaches it should brush right off. In any case it won't show. I'd like to give it a chance to dry off too. I know that horses sweat, men perspire, and women only glow, but I've been glowing hard enough to simply ruin that purple brocade."

She rose to her feet, tossing her improvised fan aside as she began to unbutton herself all the way. Longarm stared up at her, slack-jawed, and as she caught his eye in the semidarkness, she laughed and said, "Don't be silly. I'm wearing a silk shift as well as other unmentionables."

"Yes'm, but I thought ladies was supposed to keep their unmentionables unseen as well as not talked about."

"Good heavens, we're hardly at a public gathering, and it's almost dark in here anyway. You can take your shirt off too—provided you're wearing an undershirt, of course."

He wasn't. He knew he was supposed to wear something under his hickory shirt and vest, but damn it, it was summertime and bad enough that he had to wear an infernal sissy suit on the job. Like most experienced riders, he had on cotton longjohns to protect his thighs from the tobacco-brown tweed pants he wore over his boots, but he didn't think he'd mention his own unmentionables. So he just sat there, bemused, as Charity peeled off her purple dress and hung it next to her crazy hat. He didn't stare, but he could see that she did indeed have a pale pink shift still covering

37

her more or less decently. More of her upper chest and lower limbs were exposed to view than Queen Victoria might have approved in public. But she was right about them being in a private compartment, so what the hell. He told the tingle in his groin to behave itself, damn it. He'd seen more naked flesh exposed by strangers on bathing beaches in his time, and he'd managed once to go swimming with a whole posse of Mormon gals in the Great Salt Lake without going crazy. Of course, he thought as she sat down beside him, the bare shins and shoulders of those Mormon bathing beauties had been protected by the fact that it was a public bathing beach, where folks expected to see shocking expanses of flesh exposed for pure and likely healthful reasons. But sitting alone with a pair of porcelainlike bare shoulders in dusky light seemed to have an entirely different effect on a man's natural feelings.

He suspected that she hadn't expected to feel quite as intimate either, because she laughed sort of nervously as she asked him to try the window now.

He had to lean across her to do it, and that didn't help to calm him as he got a good grip on the window handle and put his back into cracking the paint. The scent of her perfume and the earthier natural odors of womankind rose between their bodies as he gritted his teeth and tried not to cuss the fool who'd painted these windows. Something had to give, and since his backbone was held together by more than dried paint, the window cracked open.

He moved back to drop into the seat next to her, and as a cool jet of sulfur-scented air lanced in under the lower edge of the drawn blinds, he said, "That'll have to do us, Miss Charity. I misdoubt that the Burlington Line finds sweeping soot off their plush a pleasant chore."

She said, "I see what you mean," as a fleck of fly ash appeared on the forearm she'd placed on the sill to cool. Then she laughed and added, "I'm glad I took my dress off. But it's cooling off in here already."

Longarm didn't answer. He supposed that, objectively, the room temperature had dropped a degree or two. But he was feeling mighty hot just the same. More light was coming in now, with the shade up a few inches. Her head and shoulders were well shaded, but the slit of sunlight across her lap revealed that the shift she wore was thin indeed. He could see the hard edges of her whalebone corset through the thin pink silk, and unless she had on a mighty tiny set of black French drawers, she was wearing nothing else betwixt her thighs. He could make out the gartered tops of her high black stockings, but from there all the way up, there seemed nothing but thigh between garters and corset, save for that mysterious dark patch that he sure hoped was black lace. Even if she was wearing shockingly skimpy black underdrawers, there was no getting around the fact that her hips were bare under that thin pink silk.

He looked away and asked, "Is it all right with you if I smoke, Miss Charity, now that there's some air in here?"

She laughed and asked, "Are you going to call me 'miss,' all the way to Deadwood?"

"Ain't taking you to Deadwood. But I'll call you anything you like as far as Casper. What did you have in mind?"

She laughed again and said, "I don't think I'd better say. The man's supposed to make the first move, isn't he?"

Longarm forgot about smoking a cheroot or anything else. He'd wondered, when she started shucking her duds, who was making what sort of move, and while he was polite enough, he knew she'd just thrown another log on the fire and that it was up to him to throw the next.

He knew that she knew most gents would have at least put an arm up on the seat behind her by now. But he had to study on it some. He didn't want a pretty gal to think he was a sissy, but he knew that if he so much as kissed her, she'd expect to go all the way with him, including to Deadwood.

His stillness seemed to puzzle her as they just rode on

a spell, listening to the clacking of the wheels and the beating of their hearts. She leaned closer as she murmured, "Penny for your thoughts, Custis?"

He grimaced and said, "My recent thoughts ain't fitting for a maiden's ears, as you've likely guessed."

"Will you tell me if I confess I'm not exactly a maiden?"

"I suspicioned you weren't exactly a frightened school-girl, and I've known about the birds and bees a spell, ah, Charity. But we'd best study our next moves before we make 'em. I know what Miss Victoria Woodhull says about you modern women, and there's a heap to be said for her liberal notions on what comes natural, but—"

Just then she twisted around, took his jaws between her cupped palms, and kissed him full on the mouth. There was nothing a gent could do in such a case but put his arms around her and kiss back. It seemed only common courtesy to run one hand down her flank in exploration; sure enough, her right hip was bare under the sensuous thin silk shift. But when they came up for air, he protested, "Damn it, there's a time and a place for everything, Charity!"

She said, "Pooh, the door is locked and this train won't arrive anywhere for hours." Then she kissed him some more and reached down and took his wrist to guide it into her lap. That dark patch under the silk was just what he'd figured it was. . . .

She spread her thighs and moaned in pleasure, thrusting her hips forward to the edge of the seat as she tried to suck his tongue out by the roots. He kept kissing her as he swung his hips off the seat to kneel between her open thighs, and he knew he wasn't taking advantage of an innocent traveling companion when she reached down between them to un-button his pants.

He was working on them with his free hand too, as she reached in to grasp his turgid shaft. "Oh, I admire tall men no matter how big they are!" she said, her breathing ragged.

He laughed and replied, "I admire a gal who knows what

40

she wants, too." And then he was in her, pounding from a kneeling position as he cupped a bare buttock in each hand while she moaned in pleasure and unbuttoned his shirt up the front.

He thought clothes were a bother at times like these, too. But it sure felt embarrassing to undress aboard a moving train in broad daylight. Of course, she was right about the door being locked, and they did have plenty of time. So they peeled down to just the corset on her and nothing worth mention on him, and stretched out on the bunk seat. The porter hadn't made it up as a bed, of course, and Charity said the plush under her bare rump tickled. But when he said there might be sheets in the top bunk's folddown, she said she liked being tickled on the ass as well as everywhere else. So they just tickled hell out of one another for a spell.

They were going at it dog-style, in time to the clacking of the train wheels, when they noticed that the train was slowing down. "Faster, darling," she said. "We don't have to stop just because the train seems to want to. I thought you said this was an express train."

He moved deeper into her, eyes closed with pleasure, as he muttered, "We must be coming into Cheyenne. We're making better time than I thought."

"How many hours before we reach Casper, dear?"

"About four, praise the Lord. But we'd best stop and behave ourselves a spell. No telling who might look in here while the train's stopped at Cheyenne."

Charity reached forward and pulled the shade down all the way as she arched her back to present her rump for deeper penetration, saying, "There. Let 'em guess what's going on in here."

But as the train slowed even more, he insisted, "We'd best get dressed. It ain't like it has to be permanent. But I mean to raise the shades whilst we're sitting in the Cheyenne yards."

"Why, darling? Do you expect to see somebody more

to your liking out on the platform?"

"Honey, they don't come any prettier than you. But I worry some about *ugly* folks. By now the gents who sent that gunslick after me back down the line have had time to learn he didn't do his job right, and while this flyer makes fair time, a telegram is even faster."

She stiffened under him as she gasped, "Oh, dear, do you expect to be intercepted at Cheyenne?"

He pulled out of her and sat up, saying, "Don't expect anything, but a man in my line of work has to be ready for expected, unexpected, and anything possible. That's why I aim to be sitting up, wearing my pants and gun, when and if somebody strides up to yon window as we're sitting in the Cheyenne yards. I'd feel dumb as hell catching a shotgun blast through a drawn curtain, wouldn't you?"

Charity sat up too, reaching by instinct for her silk shift at the head of the bunk as she gasped, "Brrr! That's frightening even to joke about! But surely if they suspected you were in here, they'd know I was too?"

"I keep telling you the folks who are agin the census ain't gentlemen, Charity," he said as he put on his shirt. "You may have some modern notions about relationships betwixt the sexes, but you're talking pure old-fashioned if you think being a she-male makes you bulletproof. Can't you get it through your pretty skull that they ain't as likely to be after *me* as after *you?*"

The train had dropped to a crawl, so they started dressing faster as she insisted, "I can't believe anyone would murder a woman just to keep from having a census taken. Can't they see that no matter how they try, the federal government's not going to rest until the population of the Dakota Territories has been counted and recorded properly?"

He strapped on his cross-draw rig, leaving his hat and frock coat hanging on the bulkhead, as he shrugged and said, "I ain't being sent to Deadwood to make 'em see the light, Charity. It's my job to make 'em stop their fool ways."

Chapter 4

He lifted the shade and sat down. They were moving into the Cheyenne yards. The compartments were on the side of the train away from the depot, so there was nothing to see at trackside but some forlorn-looking sheds and a mess of equally forlorn cows in a loading corral across the way. He considered the option of stepping out for a look-see at the crowd or lack of crowd on the station side. He decided not to bother. If anyone who was gunning for him knew he was in this compartment, he was forted up good, with a clear field of fire at the locked door, should anyone try and bust in on them. On the other hand, a tall man in a sissy brown suit made a fine target, gawking out the window of a Pullman car at people he didn't know about one way or the other.

The train stopped with a weary hiss of steam and brake air. Charity was wearing her purple dress again, and it seemed hard to believe she'd just seduced him; she tended to look prim and officious, in her duds. It must have reminded her of her own job, because she asked again about the reasons for the mysterious objections to a U.S. Census up in Deadwood.

Longarm lit a smoke and drew his .44 to rest it in his lap as he said, "Damn it, honey, if we knew their motive, we'd be halfways to arresting them."

"Can't you think of any sensible reason, darling?"

"There ain't any reason that's sensible, if their aim is permanent. You're right; sooner or later, Uncle Sam will have every hide and hair tallied in and about Deadwood. Meanwhile, there's an election coming up this November, and somebody might not want us to know how many tombstones, or just made-up voters, they have registered. Do you have one of those census forms handy?"

"No," she said. "You can't use Colorado forms in the Dakotas. Why?"

"Thought I might see something if I studied the questions folks don't seem to want to answer."

He thought back to the questions he'd been asked the previous spring, back in Denver, then he frowned and said, "Wait a spell. The jasper who come to my doorstep asked me what my race was. I told him I'd got this tan riding the High Plains, but that as far as I could tell, I was birthed a white man. Did you have to ask questions like that, Charity?"

"Of course. Race is a vital statistic. We record each person's race, age, sex, religion, occupation, and political affiliation, as you know."

"Yeah, it's starting to come back to me. They even asked if I had my own bathtub and how much money I made, now that I think back. I told them I bathed private, and that what a man makes for his honest labor is no infernal business of Washington. But that race business could lead to some interesting angles up Deadwood way. You see, it was Sioux

44

country until recent. Lots of old boys that was birthed red are working these days as cowhands, miners, dishwashers, and such. The peaceable interludes between the Indian Wars produced a mess of breeds, too. So there's a mess of folks west of the Big Muddy who might be considered either Indian or white, depending on their jobs and the duds they wear."

She nodded, but looked puzzled, so he said, "All the surviving Indians in the territories are still considered legal wards of the U.S. government. It ain't enforced, but officially, Dakota Indians are supposed to be on the set-aside reserves, or if they have the BIA's permission to work off the reservation, they have to be registered with the same."

"What's the BIA?"

"Bureau of Indian Affairs. Interior Department. Back in the days of U. S. Grant, the BIA was sort of notorious for corruption. But since Hayes cleaned up the Indian Ring, things have been run more decent."

"I don't see what Indian Affairs could possibly have to do with the U.S. Census. Indians are recorded separately."

"There you go," he said. "Indians listed as Indians don't get to vote or drink hard liquor or do half the things they might want. I've met more'n one old boy claiming to be white who sure looked sort of red around the edges. Say you were a Lakota or Cheyenne who'd decided to join the winning side and maybe had a homestead, a mining claim, a bottle of rye, or something else the Great White Father didn't think you was old enough to play with. And then say some pencil-pushing rascals was aiming to come to your dooryard asking questions about your bathtub. A thing like that could put a man off his feed and even rile him some, I reckon."

She nodded in sudden understanding and asked, "Do you think some half-breeds or full-blooded Indians are behind the mysterious business in Deadwood, then?"

He blew a smoke ring and said, "Don't know. It's one

sensible motive. But there's others, and the rascal I shot back down the line looked white enough to me."

Gazing out the window again, he muttered, "Speaking of white rascals...Change places with me, honey!"

She did as she was told, but naturally asked why. As Longarm took his seat near the window, he said. "Ain't sure. There's a couple of gents with serious-looking gun rigs trifling with those cows across the yards."

Charity craned her neck to look past him. Neither of them said anything as they watched the strangers over there for a time. Then she said, "They look like plain cowboys to me, dear. They're not doing anything, just sitting on the rails over there."

"I noticed. Facing this way. They ain't paying attention to the cows behind them, they're just sitting there in the hot afternoon sun, watching this train. You seldom see cowpokes working in the middle of a city wearing gun rigs, either. You see anything in their hands, honey?"

"No. They're just sitting there with their hands braced on the rails."

"Yeah. Men who work cows in the yards carry sticks to poke 'em with, too. That's why they call 'em cowpokes. This is getting sort of interesting. I'd sure like to ask 'em why two men dressed as range hands are taking a cowpoke sunbath. I wonder if there's time."

Just then, a distant voice valled out, *"Boooooard!"* and the bell on the locomotive commenced to ring. He shrugged and said, "We're fixing to leave Cheyenne, so we'll say no more about it."

Charity rose with a laugh and started to peel her dress off again as she said, "Good. I don't know what you've started, but I can't seem to get enough of it, you naughty thing!"

Longarm hadn't been feeling all that naughty. As she stripped down, he reached for the blind. But she said, "Leave it up. I want to make a girlish daydream come true."

He watched, bemused, as she turned, naked except for her corset and stockings, to take the plumed hat from the hook and put it on. It looked ridiculous and he told her so, laughing. She moved over to the window and crouched on the floor on her hands and knees, staring out the window in her fancy hat as the train started to move.

He laughed again as he saw what she had in mind. "Damn it, girl," he said, "we're still in the railyards, with the blinds wide open!"

"I know," she said calmly. "That's what's making me feel so wicked. I want to wave bye-bye to Cheyenne with you doing me from behind. Don't you have any sense of humor?"

"We both ought to be ashamed of our fool selves," he said. But he took off his gunbelt, dropped his pants, and knelt on the floor behind her. It felt strange as hell to be doing this in broad daylight in front of God and everybody, but it felt good too, and since all anyone could see was her head under her oversized hat, and him dressed decently behind her—if they saw him at all—he plunged into her, grabbed her corset stays, and proceeded to pleasure her to the best of his considerable ability.

Longarm survived the unexpectedly adventurous trip but as they got off the train in Casper, he was walking sort of funny, Charity Kirby was a mite stiff too. She'd told him, as they were dressing on the way into town, that she suspected she'd finally met her match. She said she was looking forward to the next leg of their journey.

That was only one of the things he had to worry about, now that he could get to a telegraph office.

He said he wanted her to wait at the depot with their possibles, but she insisted on coming along to the Western Union just down the way. So he had to check their belongings with a redcap, which was likely to cost the taxpayers another dime or more. He'd noticed that she was acting a little pensive once she had her clothes on again, with the change of trains coming up. He figured she was afraid he'd cut out on her, now that they were in Casper. He didn't tell her so, but he'd given up on the notion. Not just because they'd become such good friends, but because he could see that she was a strong-willed woman with a tendency to act on impulse, and next to having her tagging along, having her heading for Deadwood on her own was a mighty grim notion. If she at least got there safe and sound, Billy Vail had no call to blame him for anything that happened later. His orders had been to deliver her to Deadwood, not to spend the rest of his life with her.

He doubted that any man could spend the rest of a full lifetime with Charity; he wasn't sure he'd last until they reached Deadwood. But they'd worry about that later, after he saw what Western Union had to say for itself.

It had a heap. There were wires waiting there for him from the law in Derby Crossing as well as from his own Denver office. The coroner's office in Derby Crossing had decided the dead man had sort of committed suicide and that they had no call to pester Longarm further about the shootout. As an educated guess, the town constable offered the suggestion that the corpse matched the description of a professional gun called Logan Small, who'd used the same approach with better luck on a sheepherder over in Creed, Colorado, and had gotten off on self-defense when witnesses said the sheepherder had slapped leather first. Longarm filed the name away for future reference. The bully-boy approach hadn't been a good notion, going up against a known federal agent, for Small would have had a chore explaining his actions, no matter who'd won back there. On the other hand, he might have been a creature of habit and just not known how else to start a fight. The name didn't mean anything to Longarm, but that was the trouble with gunslicks. They popped up like mushrooms and generally got shot before anyone could pass their names and methods along.

The Denver office must have heard about the shootout. Billy Vail's wire told him to take good care of Miss Kirby, and that the nervous nellies back in Washington were sending some more agents out to Deadwood to find out what in thunder was going on.

Longarm balled the telegram up and threw it in the wastebasket with an annoyed frown. He'd taken care of Charity as well as he'd been able, and they hadn't answered some of the questions he'd wired them from Derby Crossing. Charity, at his side, asked, "What's wrong, darling? You look like you just received bad news."

He said, "I received *no* news worth mention. I asked old Billy to have a jaw with that rascal from your own office, the one called Boyd or Floyd or something."

"Mr. Doyle? What on earth would you want to question him about?"

"His brains, like I said in the beginning. Don't take this personal, honey. But the longer I know you, the less qualified you seem to be for the job."

"I take that personally, indeed! Don't you think I know how to read and write? Those are all the qualifications the job calls for, when you get right down to it. I told you we were all hired on a temporary basis, once every ten years."

He was aware that the clerk behind the Western Union counter was listening, so he said, "We'll talk about it later. Right now I aim to send off a few more wires, and then I'll take you to supper. Somehow that long train ride seems to have given me an appetite. How about you?"

She laughed, mollified, and moved over to study the reward posters on the wall as Longarm began to write queries on the night-letter forms.

As he scribbled in silence, Longarm heard the door open behind him. Since it was a public place, that seemed reasonable. But the metallic snick of a gun being cocked wasn't reasonable at all. So Longarm spun away from the counter in a blizzard of yellow telegraph forms, to land on one knee with his own gun drawn by the time the rascal in the doorway

49

put a .45 slug into the counter where Longarm's waistline had just been!

The first round Longarm put into the roughly dressed man in the doorway took him under the heart and staggered him back outside, with Longarm rising in hot pursuit. He didn't have far to run. The man he'd shot lay facedown on the walk outside, with one hand still gripping the big Dragoon Colt he'd used so foolishly.

The sound of gunshots at suppertime naturally attracted a crowd, and when Longarm saw a couple of men with badges and guns headed his way, he took out his wallet to flash his own silver shield at them. So everyone was putting his gun back in its holster as the three of them got to discussing the corpse on the walk.

As Longarm patiently explained his shooting of another total stranger, one of the town lawmen rolled the body over for a better look-see. Longarm knew he'd never seen the gent before, so he spotted Charity Kirby and the telegrapher staring at the scene from the Western Union doorway. They both looked a mite green about the gills. Longarm nodded and said, "You folks saw what happened. So these Casper lawmen will likely want statements from you, too."

The lawman who'd rolled the body over stood up, holding an empty wallet and a jackknife with a rabbit's foot attached to it on a little chain. He said, "If you hadn't shot him, I'd have arrested him for vagrancy. There's holes in the bottoms of his boots, and you can smell he ain't had a bath for months. Had a drinker's nose, too. Save for the gun in hand, I read him as a hobo."

Longarm nodded and said, "The gun was a hobo too. Colt hasn't made guns like that since the War. It hasn't even been converted to brass cartridges yet, for God's sake! You can buy an old pissoliver like that in any pawnshop for peanuts. But I don't reckon I'd use it to go up agin a grown man armed with a double-action .44."

The telegrapher laughed nervously, and said, "It wouldn't

have done him any good had he come after you with a Gatling, Deputy Long! Jesus, I have never seen a man your size move so sudden!" He turned to the Casper lawmen to add, "You had to be there to appreciate it, boys. It all happened in the blink of an eye. That maniac on the ground came in with the drop on the deputy here. I saw him raise and aim his gun, and before I could even shout a warning, it was all over! This big fellow moves like spit on a hot stove!"

Longarm shrugged. "Aw, mush," he said. "I heard him cocking that rusty old cap 'n ball. That's what makes 'em so cheap these days. Takes all day to thumb that hammer back. I wonder why they keep issuing such antique hardware to these boys. The last one that came after me was packing a gun old enough to vote, too."

One of the town lawmen shrugged and said, "Well, they both should of knowed better than to go up agin you, Longarm. I know I wouldn't, for we've heard of you here in Casper, and now I see they told us true about your ability to defend yourself. I'd say what we have here is another case of premeditated suicide by an obvious lunatic."

His partner nodded and asked Charity, standing pale in the doorway, if she had anything to add. The brunette licked her lips and replied, "I was looking the other way when the guns started going off. By the time I turned, it was all over. This gentleman is right about the way Deputy Long moves. As to the man at your feet, I've never seen him before, but I certainly wish somebody would put something over his face!"

The man who'd addressed her nodded and bent to place the dead man's battered hat over his face, saying, "That'll keep him until we can get him to the coroner's. I fear you all will have to come along and make a deposition for the county. It's just a formality, but we like to keep things neat in this territory."

Longarm frowned and said, "I have a train to catch to

another territory, and it leaves in less than an hour."

"It won't take that long to fill out the paperwork, Deputy."

So Longarm sighed and nodded, and between one thing and another he just made the eastbound. There hadn't been time to sup with Charity in the town of Casper after all. But she said she didn't mind, for there was a dining car on the train, and of course she insisted on coming along.

Chapter 5

They were having coffee and dessert in the dining car when Longarm suddenly frowned down at his apple pie and muttered, "They was Rip Van Winkles!"

Across the table, Charity looked up, puzzled, and he said, "Those two hombres with the antique shooting irons. We call a gent who's been in prison a long spell a Rip Van Winkle. The way the world's been changing since the War makes it hard to keep up, even when you're free to read *Scientific American* and gaze at shop windows."

"You mean you think both of those men who were after you were recently in prison?"

"Makes more sense than anything else I can come up with. Neither man was known to me, and it's my job to know at least a good description of anybody that serious about shooting folks. I've been a federal deputy for a number of years, so any professional gunslick I don't know of would have to have been out of circulation for a good spell. That would account for their choice of hardware too. The Peacemaker that most serious shootists favor these days come out in '74, and my Model T Colt .44 was invented more recent. Let's say a gent was just getting out after doing a long hard stretch for something like manslaughter or stealing horses. Anybody who'd been sent to prison maybe twenty years ago would come out considering a Patterson or Dragoon Colt a modern weapon."

She grimaced and said, "Well, they both looked shabby enough. But I'd think the last thing a man just released from prison would want to do would be to pick a fight with a federal deputy, wouldn't you?"

"Depends on the terms of their releases," he mused, adding, "I doubt that any Indians passing as registered voters would have the clout to get a man time off for good behavior and such, so we're back to political hacks. Any political machine worth its salt would have enough pull with the courts to spring a gent doing life at hard labor. And a gent doing life-at-hard would agree to most anything to get out."

He took a sip of coffee before he shook his head wearily and muttered, "That still don't answer how they knew *me*, though! In all modesty, whilst I may have a certain reputation, the pictures of federal deputies are seldom posted on walls. I know for a fact I never saw either of those gents before, yet they went for me without hesitation, like I'd been pointed out to them both ahead of time."

She nodded and said, "I see what you mean. Some member of the gang that you *would* know on sight must be following us! Do you suppose he could be aboard this train?"

"Don't know. Don't seem likely. We boarded at the last minute, and I disremember telling anybody but that telegrapher and those two Casper lawmen my immediate plans. I'll sort of walk up and down the aisle after we've ate to see what we shall see."

"What if he's in a compartment like we are, darling?"

Longarm shook his head and said, "There ain't any compartments on this infernal train, more's the pity. I asked the conductor when I signed for our passage. Later tonight they'll make up those fold-down bunks in the Pullman sections. But right now everybody aboard figures to be sitting up in public, even as you and I."

She sighed and said, "More's the pity, indeed! I was looking forward to having you for dessert!"

He shot a wary glance past her, but none of the other diners were close enough to hear them talking dirty. So he smiled and said, "You can have a second slice of pie if you like. We'd best hold off on more serious delicacies until we get to the hotel in Newcastle. We ought to be there this side of midnight."

"I don't think I can wait that long," she said. "Can't we get the porter to fix us one of those cute curtained beds?"

"Let's think practical, honey. In the first place, they won't be making up the bunks before nine or so, and in the second, you make love too noisy. There's nothing between those Pullman bunks but canvas walls."

"I'll just have to bite my tongue, then. You say this train doesn't get to our destination before midnight, and between nine and midnight would give us three whole hours."

"Hell, that's hardly time to get started with a sassy wench like you. Be a good old gal and wait till we get to Newcastle. We'll have us the rest of the night in a hotel bed. The Deadwood stage don't leave until well past sunrise."

She finished her coffee, but poured another cup from the silver pot on the white linen between them as she sighed and said, "I hope this coffee's strong. It'll have to keep me awake until I can get you out of those ridiculous pants. What do you suspect poor Mr. Doyle of, by the way?"

He blinked in surprise, then said, "Yeah, I did send a night letter to the Census Bureau to check him out, as a matter of fact. I ain't sure what I suspicion him of, but when I get to turning over rocks, I like to turn 'em *all* over."

55

"You said something about him being wrong to assign me to the Deadwood census, didn't you?"

"Well, it was you who pointed out that they only take a census every ten years. So I got to wondering what the folks who hired you do between times."

"Heavens, I never thought of that. Surely he must have some regular job with the govenment?"

"Or, like you and the other temporary help, he was hired recent. It takes political pull to land such a cushy position, Charity. I mean, what in thunder does a boss census taker have to do for his wages? You kids under him do all the legwork whilst he just sits in his office like a fat cat, with likely a secretary to forward the results to Washington. Doyle has an easier job than a postmaster or a justice of the peace, and I know for a fact that you get those positions by knowing the right people in higher places. Or by knowing somebody in the local machine who might owe you a favor or two."

She sipped her coffee thoughtfully, then put down her cup and said, "I hardly know Mr. Doyle, so I can't vouch for his character. But even if he's what you say, he's not connected with the Deadwood census. He works out of Denver, right?"

"Wrong. He's supposed to be in charge of census taking in Denver. But he sent you, a greenhorn—no offense intended—to help out and likely mess things up in Deadwood. I've been studying on that, and it won't go down my craw. Why would an office based in the state of Colorado see fit to mix in the affairs of an outfit in the Dakota Territories?"

She frowned and said, "I'll have you know I'm very good at my job, even though I'm new at it. Mr. Doyle told me they needed help in Deadwood because they were short-handed, and the Denver job was almost finished. He's not in charge of the Colorado census, by the way. I never said he was our field manager. He's some sort of assistant, I think."

Longarm frowned back as he asked, "You *think?* Don't you know? This may sound silly, but where in thunder were the two of you when this Doyle jasper told you to go to Deadwood?"

"Where were we? Why, in the Denver office, of course. We were working out of the Federal Building, the same as you people from the Justice Department. That's how come Mr. Doyle took me down the hall to see that nice Marshal Vail."

"Let's not dwell on how nice Billy Vail might be. A lady is entitled to her opinions, I reckon. Are you saying this Doyle rascal waylaid you in the census office and just led you down to ours, informal-like?"

She pursed her lips in thought and then nodded and said, "As a matter of fact, that's sort of the way it was, now that I think about it. Are you suggesting Mr. Doyle could have been an imposter?"

"I'll know better after I get the answers to some wires I just sent, back in Casper. After this Doyle introduced you to my boss, and Vail agreed we'd be pleased as punch to see you safe to Deadwood, did you go back into your office to jaw about it with your fellow workers, or did you run home to pack your things, seeing as the northbound flyer was leaving sudden?"

"As a matter of fact, I did go straight to my hotel to pack and check out! But, darling, what you're suggesting sounds so wild! I knew Mr. Doyle; at least I'd seen him around the office. I didn't know what he did there until he told me, but—"

"So he could have been a temporary employee like you, or even just a gent who liked to hang about the Federal Building, since everybody working for the census was new in Denver and could have taken him for a member of the courthouse gang. Don't look so green about the gills, honey. If he slickered Billy Vail too, he must have been a powerful talker."

Charity shook her head, waving her egret feathers wildly, and said, "It doesn't make sense, dear. I can see how it's possible I was tricked into leaving for Deadwood by some sort of confidence man, but what on earth would be the point? If I've been sent on some sort of foolish snipe hunt, I'm sure to find out as soon as I reach Deadwood and talk to the others. So what motive could he have had for playing such a grotesque joke?"

Longarm took out an after-supper cheroot and lit up as he studied on her words. He blew some smoke out his nostrils before he said, "You're right. It don't make sense. If the folks in Deadwood are expecting you, I'm just a suspicious-natured cuss and we'll say no more about it. If they *ain't* expecting you, they won't let you take any census, so you can't cause any problems for them, so that can't be the plan. Maybe this Doyle jasper just had some reason for getting you out of Denver."

She thought about that for a moment, then replied, "No, I told you I'd about finished my job in Denver and I'd already gotten my two weeks' notice. So I was planning on going back East in any case."

She put her toe against his under the table and added, "I'm glad I met you first, though. Whether Mr. Doyle is a legitimate supervisor or some kind of lunatic, I owe him a lot."

Longarm laughed and said that made two of them. Then he helped her to her feet and they went back to their Pullman seats in the next car back. He told Charity to stay put and knit or something while he ran a patrol the length of the train. She said she'd miss him and to hurry, so he did. He strode down the aisle as if he were going somewhere important, and nobody seemed to pay him much mind, except for a small boy sitting with a decent-looking blonde. "Look, Mama, a cowboy!" the kid piped up as he strode past.

They were likely Easterners. Anyone could see he wasn't dressed right for working cows. He might have been, had it been up to him to dress comfortably instead of gussied up like a dude in this infernal frock coat and tie. If any of the other passengers thought he looked cow, they didn't see fit to comment on it out loud. Nobody said anything at all as he passed. He checked each face out as he did so, not letting on he was interested.

Longarm had a photographic memory for faces he'd seen on a reward poster or at the other end of a gun. But by the time he got to the observation car at the rear of the train, he hadn't seen anybody suspicious.

He stepped out on the empty observation platform to make sure it *was* empty. It was fairly dark now, so there wasn't much to see back down the track. The train was doing maybe forty miles an hour, so nobody was following them aboard mortal horseflesh, either. He shrugged, turned around, and retraced his steps to where he'd left Charity.

When he got there, he saw that she'd tipped the porter to make up the berth they'd hired. He couldn't tell what the other passengers in the car were thinking, but not another bunk had been made up and curtained for the night. Charity smiled brightly at his red face and said, "I told the porter I was tired, dear."

"I noticed," he said.

It was more embarrassing to just stand there blushing like a bride than to climb in with her, so he did, saying, "Dammit, woman, it's barely eight o'clock yet!"

She giggled as she put her hat in the net stretched across the windows and began to shuck her duds, kneeling on the mattress. "I know. I couldn't wait. Help me out of this damned dress. It's awkward, undressing all scrootched up like this!"

He'd have done anything to keep her quiet, so he helped her peel, all too aware of the others just outside the thin canvas curtains, who were doubtless wondering what she was giggling about. He got her down to her corset and stockings, and as she unhooked her high-button shoes, with

59

her shapely legs drawn up, he had to admit she made a tempting picture. It was not too dark in their little canvas cave to see her, all over, for lamplight spilled over the top of the folded canvas hangings. He looked for some way to fasten the infernal canvas shut. There was no way to lock the door, since there wasn't any door, but he found some buttons and that made him feel better. At least the infernal curtains wouldn't part of their own accord.

She put her shoes in the net and started clawing at his buttons, begging him to hurry in a whisper he was sure they could hear back in the observation car. He whispered back, "Hush, girl! I'll do anything you want, if you'll only keep it down to a roar!"

So she laughed and rolled over on her back, legs spread in welcome as he awkwardly got out of his duds. He'd never felt so naked before as he thought about the eyes that were probably fixed on the mysterious green canvas from just across the aisle and all up and down the car. But the fat was in the fire anyway, and he knew she'd start whispering dirty again any minute, so he rolled into the saddle and put his lips to her ear to whisper, "Now not a damned word, Goddamm it!" as he entered her.

She hissed like a boiling-over teakettle and dug her nails into his bare rump as she arched her pelvis up to meet his thrusts, with her heels dug into the mattress for purchase. He knew she was enjoying the near-public passion like the dirty little kid she was at heart, but at least she was discreet enough not to give the other passengers a blow-by-blow description of what he was doing to her. Longarm figured they could likely guess, and he had to admit, it added a certain spice to the action. But enough was enough, and when he sensed that she was about to yell, he clapped a palm over her mouth, so they both came with her chewing hell out of his hand.

He managed to climax quietly, having had practice in his youth on a porch swing, with the gal's menfolk just inside. As they both relaxed in each other's arms, grinning like two kids playing hooky, a childish voice piped up, "Whatcha doin', mister?"

Longarm turned his head to see that a little kid had stuck his cute infernal head in between the curtains and was staring at their naked forms with considerable interest. He sighed and said, "Go back to your own seat and behave yourself, sonny. Me and the missus is trying to go to sleep, see?"

"You don't look like you're sleeping, mister. You look like you're hurting the lady."

Before Longarm could protest his innocence, a woman's voice on the far side of the canvas called out, "David Boggs, you come away from there this very instant! Haven't I told you not to pester strangers, you wicked child?"

Little David's face disappeared, but then the whole damned car started laughing when his distant voice piped up, "The cowboy and the lady was rasslin', Mama. He must have been winning, for he was on top."

The only bright spot in the whole dismal business was the distant sound of a hard slap to somebody's deserving face. Longarm muttered, "I hope she tore his head off. Jesus, what'll we do now, honey?"

Charity kissed him and whispered, "I want to get on top. If he comes back, he'll say I'm winning, right?"

"I don't think I'm up to it," he said, even as he rolled over onto his back. "No offense. Getting caught in the act by that angelic little bastard seems to have cooled me down a mite."

He'd underestimated her abilities, however. After some tender ministrations to his wilting manhood, he found himself rising eagerly to the occasion. She looked right pretty, kneeling above him like that, with her head bobbing up and down over his groin. . . .

Chapter 6

They ate ham and eggs for breakfast. Longarm washed his down with three cups of strong black coffee, for he hadn't gotten much sleep. When they'd finished, Longarm parked Charity under a rubber tree in the hotel lobby and told her to stay put and keep her duds on while he found out about the stage to Deadwood. He saw no need to worry her by mentioning his other plans, which included a stop at the Western Union and the local marshal's office. While he was about it, a quick patrol of the town wouldn't hurt. At this hour there were few people on the streets, and most of the saloons wouldn't open until noon. Newcastle was as small a trail town as it sounded like, and so strangers tended to stand out.

The Western Union office had some answering wires waiting for him. He sent one to Billy Vail, telling him where he was and that he was still breathing, before he read what the Census Bureau had to say about their Mr. Doyle.

The Census Bureau didn't have a thing to say about anyone named Doyle. They'd never heard of him. The name wasn't on the Denver payroll. Longarm nodded thoughtfully and sent them some more questions.

His office had sent him a negative report on the man he'd gunned in Casper, as well. There were no wants or warrants out on a man answering his description. Longarm had already sent one wire to Billy Vail, so he wired the Washington office, asking them to check on anyone who'd checked out of prison recently with a gold tooth and an old knife scar on his left cheek. He suggested they concentrate on long-term felons who might have been sprung unexpectedly early. He knew it was a blind lead if either of the rascals had done time in some state or territorial prison, but it was all he could think of this early in the morning.

He went next to the town marshal's office. The boss wasn't in yet, but the deputy holding the desk on the floor with his boot heels offered the negative help that as far as he knew, no hardcased-looking strangers seemed to be lurking in or about the fair city of Newcastle. He said, "We have us a vagrancy statute, being as we're on the railroad, and Lord only knows who might hop off a passing freight to menace our chickens and womenfolk. If anybody strange but respectable's slipped past my eye of late, you'd be likely to find them checked into the hotel. There ain't but one hotel that hires rooms to transients."

Longarm nodded and said, "I know. I spent the night there. And there ain't anybody else new in town. I checked that out with the room clerk."

The deputy shrugged. "There you go. Who are you looking for, Longarm?"

"Nobody in particular. Just wanted to make sure I was neither followed nor staked out. My real case seems to be in Deadwood, but some folks seem not to want me to get there. I seem to have foxed 'em by getting off at this unexpected stop, so me and my, ah, fellow federal agent will just hop the Deadwood stage and say no more about it. You wouldn't know when the stage figures to pull out, would you?"

The deputy nodded and said, "Sure I would. She leaves for Deadwood in about half an hour, if my watch is right and Calamity is sober."

"Calamity?"

"Calamity Jane Canary. She's the one driving the Deadwood stage."

"You got to be greening me!"

"No I ain't. Old Calamity's a tolerable stage jehu, considering. I know some folks think it ain't natural for no female to jehu no stage, but what the hell, Calamity Jane ain't a natural female, neither."

Longarm laughed and said, "I noticed that, when I met her at Madame Moustache's in Dodge a spell back. I met her as a lawman, not as a customer, by the way."

The deputy laughed and said, "I never suspicioned you of being that desperate, old son. She couldn't have been much to look at even when she was younger and hadn't caught the clap. Anyhow, that's who they got driving the Deadwood stage these days. Like I said, she's a tolerable jehu, sober. She can cuss a mule better than most, even if she was birthed female."

"It beats walking, I reckon," Longarm said with a sigh. "I'll pick up my sidekick and possibles and see if the old bawd aims to get us there or not."

He went back to the hotel, and between them, he and Charity got their gear down to the livery where the stage was said to start from. They didn't see any stage when they got there. The black hostler lounging in the door nudged a mail sack at his feet with a toe and told them it was bound for Deadwood, so Calamity Jane hadn't lit out yet.

The sun was rising and there was no decent place to sit and wait. Longarm took out a cheroot and swore softly as he lit it. Charity asked what was keeping the stage, and he said, "Don't know. The jehu is an ugly alcoholic nymphomaniac, as well as a born liar. So even when and if she gets here, we'll never know for sure."

Charity said, "I've heard of Calamity Jane. I think I read about her in some magazine."

He snorted in disgust and said, "You shouldn't read books like that. Ned Buntline sort of made old Calamity up for his Wild West magazine, and she's crazy enough to believe it's really her he's talking about."

She laughed and asked, "Who *is* he talking about, then?"

"Don't know. Ned Buntline is a mighty funny fellow. You see, he makes up tales about the country out here from whole cloth. But for some infernal reason, he uses the names of real people in his crazy adventure yarns. I was talking to old Bill Cody about it one time, and Bill thinks it's sort of amusing. He says he don't mind being called Buffalo Bill, and that his friends all know he never acted that crazy in real life."

"Good heavens, everyone knows who Buffalo Bill is! Are you saying he's a big fake?"

"He is and he isn't, honey. Bill Cody's shot his share of buffalo and Indians and he really rode for the Pony Express and all, as a kid. He's a tolerable scout and a damned fine marksman. Rides a horse pretty, too. But that infernal Ned Buntline has written a whole mess of pennydreadfuls having Buffalo Bill do wonders that just never happened."

He stepped out in the roadway to peer either way for their tardy stage. Then he rejoined her and added, "Jim Hickok got killed by Ned Buntline's stories."

"You mean Wild Bill Hickok?"

"His name wasn't Bill, Wild or otherwise. He was baptized James Butler Hickok, back in the Midwest. Buntline started writing yarns about him after he saw how well his Buffalo Bill bull was selling back East."

65

"But you say this Buntline person killed him?"

"Yep. Officially, Jim was shot in the back by Cockeyed Jack McCall, a half-witted young saddle tramp, up in Deadwood, where we're headed. But the reason McCall shot Hickok was that he'd read all sorts of garbage in the Wild West magazines they found later amongst his possibles. McCall thought Hickok was the top gun in the West and that if he shot him, McCall would likely find himself on the cover of Ned Buntline's magazines and maybe be invited East to tour in vaudeville shows like Buffalo Bill and even Hickok, one time. Of course, what he wound up appearing on was the business end of a hangman's rope, but Ned Buntline forgot to put that part in his so-called Code of the West."

The stablehand called out, "Hyar she comes!"

But Longarm already knew what a six-mule stagecoach sounded like, coming around a corner, so he'd moved himself and Charity out of the way by the time the battered old Concord, driven by a battered figure in men's duds a size too big, braked to a stop in a cloud of dust in front of them. The short, stout jehu hauled back on the reins, yelling, "I said whoa and I mean whoa, you lop-eared, fucking jackrabbit bastards!"

Longarm called up, "Watch your mouth, Miss Canary. Ladies present."

Calamity Jane stared owlishly down at them for a moment. Then her dusty, dreadful face cracked open in a broad, roguish grin and she yelled, "Hot rocks in my britches! Is that really you, Longarm? I thought they'd stuffed and mounted you as a relic of the old times in Dodge by now!"

He said, "Not yet. We'll be riding your fair chariot to Deadwood at public expense, Miss Jane. This here's Miss Charity Kirby, and before you say anything dumb, she's a federal agent, like my own self."

Calamity Jane nodded down at Charity and said, "How do. You're good-looking enough to work the cribs at the

Silver Dollar or the Alhambra, but I'll take the man's word you're an amateur. You two want to ride up here with me, or down in the coach?"

Charity looked dubiously up at the high, swaying driver's seat and said she'd just as soon take her chances down below. So Calamity Jane called the stablehand a lazy nigger bastard and he threw the mail sack up to her, growling under his breath, "My mammy and my pappy was black, but they was married, and neither of them had the clap, either."

She didn't hear it. She was, mercifully, a little deaf as well as too cracked to notice the looks and comments she drew in passing.

She called down, "Well, get aboard unless you aim to chase me on foot, goddamm it!" So Longarm helped Charity into the coach. But as he was about to follow, Calamity Jane called down, "Climb up here and jaw a spell with me, Longarm. As you see, I've no shotgun rider, and there's been some trouble on the road ahead."

He looked in at Charity, who smiled and said, "Go on and see what she wants, darling. I'm pretty sure I can trust even *you,* with anyone that ugly!"

So he swung up to join Calamity Jane as the old bawd cracked her reins and said, "What are you waitin' for, you sons of bitches? Move your lazy asses afore I lash 'em raw and set fire to your infernal tails!"

The team lunged forward in the traces as if their lives depended on it—which might indeed have been the case, for as they tore down the street at a dangerous clip, Calamity Jane threw jagged hunks of railroad ballast at their frantic rumps and shouted obscene threats to their continued existence.

Longarm steadied himself on the wildly swaying seat as he growled, "Take it easy, Miss Jane. You don't have to show off for me, and the lady down below has delicate ears."

Calamity Jane stopped throwing rocks, but as she settled

down to just whipping the rumps of the rear mules with her loose reins, she sniffed and said, "I'll bet she'd be delicate. That's a gal who likes to give French lessons if ever I've met one. 'Fess up, Longarm, what are you doing, traveling with a whore? I thought you was too proud to pay for pussy. That's what you told me that time in Dodge, remember?"

He remembered. God, had it only been such a few short years? Even as the new girl at Madame Moustache's, Jane Canary had not been pretty. But she'd been sort of country-fresh, considering the line she was in, and while her career had lasted, she'd been popular enough. It was awesome to consider how venereal disorders and more liquor than the human system was designed to absorb could mess up a reasonably desirable girl's body and brain.

They swung out of town and headed north-northeast, and as the mules settled to a more sensible trot, he asked her how long it should take them to make Deadwood.

"We ought to make her to Pleasant Valley Station by sundown," she said. "That's where we'll be stopping for the night. You want to get laid?"

"Damn it, Miss Jane, it's no more'n fifty miles from Newcastle to Deadwood."

"I know. Wait till you see the wicked trail ahead. I dasn't drive after dark in the Black Hills, so we're making her in two easy legs. You never answered when I asked if you wanted to get laid, honey bun."

"Uh, not hardly, Miss Jane."

"Call me Calamity. I'm used to it, even if I did think it was sort of mean of the boys in Dodge to hang the handle on me when I caught a dose. I've been cured of the clap, by the way."

"Uh, I'm glad to hear that, Calamity."

"Yeah, it left me with a little rheumatiz when the weather's damp. But my old ring-dang-doo is clean as a whistle and waiting for the right man to come along and fill it."

"I sure thank you for your complimentary offer, Calamity. But if it's all the same with you, I'll take a rain check for now."

"You're screwing that sassy brunette down there in the purple outfit, eh?"

"Now what makes you say such a thing as that, Calamity?"

"Hell, every man's screwing somebody, if he's turning it down. Besides, that stuck-up little gal would screw a snake, did she get someone to hold its head for her. I can always tell a wild and wicked young gal, honey bun. I used to be one, you know."

He didn't answer. He did know. He knew that women were better at sizing up their own kind than men were, too. Calamity Jane was right on the money about Charity being wild and wicked. He'd find out what else she was when they got to Deadwood.

"Listen, Calamity," he said, "you can make a measly fifty miles in one day if you put your mind to it."

She shook her head as she pointed with her jaw at the grade ahead and said, "I ain't pulling this coach, them poor ignorant mules is. Do they look like Pony Express mounts to you? This stage line is running on a shoestring, with worn-out critters and running stock they ought to sell for kindling wood. You can see how many passengers we carry, now that there's a rail connection into Deadwood. How come you got off back there instead of Edgemont, where you could have took the train? That's what ever'body else seems to be doing these days."

He said, "I don't aim to approach Deadwood like everybody else. I've had two shootouts getting this far. But I never allowed for two whole days on the stage."

She whistled under her breath and said, "I might have knowed you was here on serious business. Who are you after, honey bun? I ain't seen many of the old Wild Bunch up in Deadwood of late. Things has been kind of slow since the mines started bottoming out. At the rate things is going, we'll soon have us a ghost town."

She was silent a moment, then went on, "Ghosts and me seem to be all that's left of the old crowd. Did you read that piece in the papers about me keeping up Jim's grave? They took them a picture of me weeding his plot, and when the wolf wind comes down of a winter to heave the tombstones outten the frosted earth, I put Jim's back, standing straight like he'd want it."

He sighed and said, "I saw the item in the *Police Gazette*, and you ought to be ashamed of yourself for greening those reporters so. You've no call to tell folks you were Hickok's sweetheart, Calamity. It ain't decent, with his wife and family still living."

She sniffed and said, "Well, dammit, he did like me a mite. He bought me a drink in the Buckhorn one time. Said it was the least he could do for an old gal from Dodge. We was both in Dodge at the same time, you know."

"I know, Calamity. He was a police officer and you was, ah, in another line of work."

"Jim never let on that he looked down on me for being a soiled dove. I swear, he was friendly as anything to me, right up to the day he died. Did you read about me swearing to avenge my sweetheart's death in *Ned Buntline's True Tales of the West?*"

"I did, and I was sort of disgusted, Calamity. Cockeyed Jack was hung for the killing fair and square. Nobody avenged Jim Hickok, least of all you, and it still ain't right for you to go about telling folks he was sweet on you."

"Suppose I told you he made love to me one night, when we was both drunk and his wife had a headache?"

He shook his head wearily and said, "You forget I knew Jim too, no offense. I'll allow he could get crazy drunk on occasion, but headache or no, his wife was a handsome woman."

She cackled and said, "Well, mebbe after a man's been

70

eatin' steak for a spell, a bowl of beans strikes his fancy. I'll allow I had to get him drunk to do it, but—"

"Hush up and drive, damn it," he cut in. He figured it behooved decent folk not to speak ill of the dead, and if James Butler Hickok had ever gotten that drunk, it was just as well the matter lay buried with him. He'd likely turn over in his grave if he knew Calamity Jane was telling such awful tales about him.

She said, "Well, I don't care if you mean to sleep with that skinny brunette instead of a real woman tonight, for I've had me a real man in my time, and it'd likely split me like a cedar log at my age if you was hung half as good. I noticed you had a Winchester strapped to that army saddle of your'n. When I rest the mules atop the grade, you'd best fetch it up here for comfort."

"What do I need a carbine for, Calamity?"

"Road agents, of course. I told you we'd been having trouble with 'em on this run."

"You mean someone's taken to holding up near-empty stages?"

"Not yet. The last time they tried to stop me, I fit 'em off."

He eyed her suspiciously and asked, "With what, rocks?"

She reached her free hand inside her shabby overcoat and produced a sixgun that belonged in a museum. "This old Walker don't throw rocks, honey bun. It was made for killing Comanche, and I reckon I showed them there was life in the old gal yet."

He nodded, unconvinced, as she put the old cap-and-ball revolver away. He knew Calamity Jane was given to lying when the truth was in her favor.

"I don't suppose you hit any of the men who attacked the stage, huh?" he asked.

"I didn't put any on the ground," she said, "but I might have winged a couple, if that's what you mean."

That had indeed been what he'd meant. But to comfort

71

her, the next time they stopped to rest the mules at the top of a grade, he climbed down and got inside with Charity to get his Winchester. Charity kissed him and said, "It's lonesome down here. Have you ever done it in a stage-coach?"

"No," he lied. "We're going to be stopping for the night, so hold your horses. I got to talk some more, topside."

"What on earth are the two of you talking about? Is she trying to make goo-goo eyes at you?"

He laughed incredulously, and said, "Wouldn't do her any good if she was. I'm just trying to pick up on Deadwood gossip, honey. She's been there since the original gold strike. So between her lies there's some facts and figures. Like the fact that Deadwood's starting to lose population."

"Do you think that would be of interest to the census?"

"Be of interest to the electoral college this November, if they've been padding the population figures up ahead. I got to get back up. We'll jaw some more about it tonight."

He climbed up by Calamity Jane as she threw some more rocks at her mules to move them down the next grade at a dead run. "Take it easy, damn it! You'll tip us over!" he yelled.

But she laughed loudly and answered, "Never have, so far, and I always run 'em along this stretch. Who's driving this infernal Concord, you or me?"

Fair was fair, so he shut up and just hung on as well as he was able until, sure enough, they arrived at the bottom on all four wheels and gravity slowed the mules down to a safer trot up the far grade.

They rode on for what felt like a year or so, with him asking questions and Calamity Jane talking wild and driving even wilder. She seemed to have forgotten that when he'd met her in Dodge as a young trail hand, right after the War, she'd only been a few years older than him, and that he was still on the friendly side of forty. To hear Calamity Jane tell it, she'd led Lewis and Clark over the Shining Mountains and showed Jim Bridger where to find the Great Salt Lake. He wasn't impolite enough to ask a lady her age, so he didn't know how old she really was. But at the rate she was going, she'd soon look old enough to have shown Dan'l Boone the way through the Cumberland Gap—and slept with him too, to hear her tell it.

By the time they were coming to the first stage stop, he'd about given up trying to pan some nuggets of information from the sand and rocks of useless legends. The company outpost was a sprawl of country-rock walls and lodgepole-and-sod roofing, surrounded by a pole corral and livestock. They kept more pigs and chickens than mules, and the mules they had looked mighty weary already.

Calamity Jane pulled off the wagon trace in front of the rambling wreckage and braked the stage to a dusty stop, yelling, "First stage to Deadwood. There's water in yon pump and the shithouse is out back. Drink your fill and shit your damnedest by the time I change teams, or I'll leave you here with these niggers!"

Longarm stayed put with the Winchester across his knees as he wondered why she called the station hands niggers. There were two of them. One looked like he was perhaps half Lakota, and the other was a white man of about forty with shifty eyes and a drinking look to him.

Calamity Jane climbed down to circle the stone building, heading for the sanitary facilities. Her kidneys led a rough life. Charity stuck her plumed head out the window below to ask what was going on. "We're changing the team," Longarm called down.

"So soon? We're only a few miles from Newcastle."

"Yeah, well, that's why they call these things stagecoaches. The stages have to be set close in rough country like this. Do you need to use the, ah, facilities?"

She grimaced and said, "Not after that . . . woman," and ducked back inside. He smiled thinly as he realized what she meant. He didn't think it could be true that you could catch a dose from a toilet seat, for he'd have done so for sure by now, considering some of the places he'd been. But it was sort of distasteful to consider crapping after Calamity.

The station hands had swapped teams by the time Calamity came back into view, holding a brown paper bag to her face. She lowered it with a sigh and put it in the side pocket of her coat as she approached, grumbling, "Well, you boys sure took your own sweet time. How am I to run on any sort of schedule if you shilly-shally with my mules?"

The breed frowned and walked away, muttering to himself. Calamity Jane grinned at the white one and said, "You must be new on the line, for I don't think we've screwed yet."

The man flinched like somebody'd dropped a frog down the back of his shirt and followed the breed, calling out, "You're right, Jim. She's as loco as you said she was."

Calamity Jane climbed up beside Longarm and cackled, "I likes to shake the new hands up. I wouldn't really screw him. He's old and ugly."

She punctuated her statement by zinging a piece of ballast at the off-mule's rump, and they were off and running. The sun was getting higher, so the still, dry air was getting warmer. Longarm took off his frock coat and folded it between his spine and the seatback. Then he took the damned tie off and opened his shirt while he was at it.

He wondered how Charity was making out down below. They were alone on the trail and would be for hours. It'd probably be safe for her to take off her purple dress and ride more comfortably in her shift, but he didn't yell any suggestions down. He knew Charity needed little advice when it came time to shuck her duds. He wondered why that thought was giving him a hard-on. He'd had her that morning, every way but flying, but making love to Charity was like eating salted peanuts in a taproom.

For a crazy woman, Calamity Jane was good at reading minds. She said, "This next stretch is sort of tedious. You

74

could swing down and get some slap-and-tickle whilst I drive, if you like. I promise I can't peek, sitting up here like this."

"Jesus," he growled, "don't you ever think of anything else, Calamity?"

She laughed and said, "Hell, what else is there to think about, when you get right down to cases? Screwing makes the world go 'round, honey bun. I reckon I've screwed a thousand men and I still ain't had my fill. How about you?"

"I've never screwed even *one* man, Calamity."

She turned to face him and slapped him on the thigh with her free hand. "You don't know what you've been missing!" she laughed. Then she turned her head further to add with a frown, "Oh-oh, look back yonder."

He did, and muttered, "Aw, hell, somebody has to be joking!"

"Joke or no, that's an Injun smoke signal, Longarm."

"When you're right, you're right, Calamity," he admitted as he stared at the white puffs drifting in the cobalt-blue sky above the ridge behind them.

These far-flung foothills of the main Black Hills massif were nearly bare of timber, but there were more boulders all about for cover than a man liked to study on. He swung around to face forward as he levered a round into the Winchester's breech and said, "If that's real and not just some kids playing Indian, the smoke talk's meant for someone up the trail a piece. You know this wagon trace better than me, Calamity. Where would you stake yourself out if you was a Lakota?"

"Don't know. I ain't a Lakota. I thought the rascals was all supposed to be over in Pine Ridge, now that they don't own these parts no more."

He said, "Most of them are. I was over on the Sioux reserve on another case a spell back. I reckoned things was pretty well cooled off for now. Have you been having Indian trouble up this way of late?"

She shook her head. "Last full-blood I've seed about Deadwood was swamping out a saloon for drinking money. The army cleared these hills of Sioux back in '76. Leastways they said they had. What do you figure we ought to do, Longarm?"

He thought for a moment, then said, "Well, the first thing that comes to mind would be wheeling this rig around and making a beeline back to Newcastle, picking up them station hands on the fly. On the other hand, we know that whoever's making that smoke talk is between here and town. They could be signaling someone up ahead to do something surly, or they could be playing Halloween tricks on us, or, like I said, they could be some kids from town just playing games. I'm having a hard time getting used to the idea of Indians in the Black Hills at this late date."

"I ain't afeared of any redskin birthed of mortal woman," said Calamity Jane, whipping the mules to a faster trot.

It had already been established that she was crazy, so Longarm kept silent.

But he aimed to get to Deadwood, one damned way or another, and since it was six of one and half a dozen of the other, he didn't insist on going back. He didn't know if she could hit anything with that old hogleg under her coat, but he had a lot of .44-40 rounds across his lap, and how many Indians could there be in these parts?

They topped a rise and he stood up in the boot, bracing himself with his free hand for a look ahead. The next draw seemed empty enough, save for the boulders all around. Calamity Jane took advantage of the downslope to lash the mules to a run, sitting him down hard as he yelled, "Take it easy!" while the coach swayed wildly from side to side, with its wheels touching ground only occasionally.

Charity leaned out the window to yell, "For God's sake, has she gone crazy?"

Longarm yelled back, "Yeah, a long time ago. Hang on to the straps beside the seat, honey. Calamity, if you don't slow down, I'm going to have to shoot you or worse."

But before Calamity Jane could answer, let alone slow down, a rifle spanged, and what sounded like a big angry hornet buzzed past Longarm's Stetson while another slug from another rifle thunked into the planking near his shins. The mules were spooked by the fusillade and naturally ran off the trail. The coach hit a knee-high rock with its off-front wheel and Calamity gasped, "Thunderation! We're going over!"

She was telling the truth for once. Longarm rolled to the high side as the coach fell sideways to land on its side with a horrendous crash in a cloud of dust and spinning wheels. The mules busted free and kept going, still tethered in a bunch. Longarm wound up flat in the dust and stunned, but still hanging on to his Winchester as he rolled behind a boulder, trying to get his bearings. He saw somebody in blue denim coming at him through the mustard-colored haze, and since he knew it couldn't be either Charity or Calamity Jane, he put a bullet in the son of a bitch, folding him like a jackknife around his belt buckle. Behind him, Calamity Jane's big hogleg roared like a baby cannon, and he heard her yell, "Bust my britches, I *got* the shit-eatin' dog!"

He heard the clatter of steel-shod hooves on stone scree so he jumped to his feet and staggered clear of the dust cloud in time to see two riders and four ponies heading up the far slope as if the devil were in hot pursuit. He took aim and fired, but of course at that range he missed, and then the bastards were over the ridge and gone.

He turned around. The dust was starting to settle. He saw Calamity Jane on the far side of the spilled coach, holding her old Walker up like she was fixing to have a duel. He called out, "See if Miss Charity's all right. I'll have a look at the one I put on the ground."

"I got another on this side, when you finish scalping *him!*" Calamity called back. Longarm walked over to where the man he'd shot lay half hidden by a boulder. He moved in gingerly, holding his Winchester ready for sudden moves. But as soon as he got a good look, he saw that the road agent was as dead as he ever figured to get. The man lay on his side, sort of chewing on a fist-sized rock, with his open mouth drooling blood. Longarm knelt and grounded the Winchester to pat the corpse down. There wasn't any identification on him. The stranger had some loose change in his jeans and a couple of cigars in a shirt pocket. The rifle he'd dropped nearby was an old Spencer repeater, of the sort the BIA issued the Indians for hunting, to the army's considerable anguish. But the dead man was no Indian. He'd just been playing Indian with smoke signals and a BIA gun. He was a white man of about forty.

Longarm helped himself to the smokes as he thought about the lack of ID on this fellow, and compared him to the other two he'd helped on their way to Judgment recently. A man wandering free for any length of time at all picks up stuff to fill his pockets with—poker chips, scraps of paper—and this jasper was wearing a new denim outfit, too.

"Hell, old son," Longarm said to the late bushwhacker, "you ain't been out of the pokey long enough to matter. You should have quit whilst you was ahead."

Then Calamity called out to him, and she sounded anxious. He rose and headed toward where she stood atop the overturned coach. She was looking down through the open door. As he approached, she said, "Your girlfriend 'pears to be hurt, Longarm."

He clambered up on top of the coach and handed her his Winchester. "Watch the skyline," he told her as he lowered himself through the door. Charity was sprawled on the downside wall, and he hunkered down beside her. He touched her gently, and she opened her eyes.

"I feel so funny," she said weakly.

"You ought to, honey," he said. "You've been shot."

He didn't tell her how bad it looked. The blood flowing freely from a hole at her waistline was dark and plentiful. He checked her pulse, which was weak and ragged. She should have been dead by now. But she licked her lips and said, sounding annoyed, "That's impossible. . . . They weren't supposed to shoot *me*. . . ."

He nodded soberly and said, "I know. It might have been an accident. On the other hand, they might have gotten to wondering if you'd changed sides after I managed to shoot my way out of two setups. You want to tell me about it, Charity? It ain't like you'll be going to jail, and what the hell, we had us some good times together, remember?"

She smiled up at him and said, "Do I ever. I never meant to get attached to you, darling, but I've always been a sucker for broad shoulders. How did you figure it out?"

"Didn't take much figuring, once I studied on that purple dress and white egret plumes. Like I said, they don't post pictures of federal agents. A lot of gents fit my general description, but a man traveling with a lady dressed so unusual ain't hard to spot. I was hoping at first that you was just too inexperienced to wear a duster like most traveling gals. But you slipped up in other ways. You didn't know that the Census Bureau uses the same standard form all over. You didn't know what the BIA was, even though you claimed to be working for a branch of the Interior Department, and even though you covered yourself pretty slick, it only took a couple of wires to find out that nobody named Doyle works in the Denver office. You and him slickered Billy Vail, but you failed to slicker me. I was waiting till we got to Deadwood to have it out with you about the way you made a point of showing that egret hat at the window in the Cheyenne railyards, but since time is of the essence, you'd best tell me now who you've been working for, Charity."

She had blood on her teeth as she smiled sort of wickedly and asked, "Why should I?"

He said, "You may not think you owe me, but they just shot you, honey. Don't you want to pay the rascals back?"

She didn't answer; she just lay there, smiling up at him like a wicked kid in church. He moved his hand in front of her eyes, then felt her pulse again. "Shit," he muttered, and closed her dead eyes. Then he rose to climb out of the coach. "Well, Calamity," he said as he emerged, "I told you we'd turn over. Now how in thunder are we going to get there?"

Calamity said, "If we can corner them mules grazing up on the ridge, we can ride 'em back to the last station and get the boys to help us right her. I've turnt over afore, and nothing's busted serious. How's that gal of your'n?"

"She's dead. The reason I ain't crying is because she was in on it with them, and the infernal woman died before she could tell me who shot her."

"Well, I'll screw you if you ain't got nothing better to do."

"I got something better to do, Calamity. You stay here. I'll go round up the mules."

Chapter 7

It came as no great surprise to discover that the white man back at the stage station no longer seemed to be working for the line. The breed who ran the spread said he'd taken off shortly after they'd left, adding, "He only worked here a couple of days. Come down the trail to say the line had sent him to help out. I don't know where in hell he went."

Longarm said, "I do. He went to send a smoke signal as soon as he saw those egret plumes they'd told him to watch for. The other side's playing more serious than I figured. They thought of covering every infernal way into Deadwood, after all."

They all sat down inside and had a couple of drinks to steady their nerves and fortify themselves for the job ahead. Calamity was sure the three of them could lever the coach back aboard its wheels. The two men weren't so sure. But after he'd studied on it some, the breed said he'd hitch up the buckboard out back, and that with some lodgepoles and the block and tackle from the stable, they might work something out.

The three of them took the buckboard and gear back to the stage, leading a fresh team. The breed had said they could leave the dead gal with him, and that he'd run her into the coroner's in Newcastle. But when they got back to the stage, Charity's body was missing.

Calamity Jane asked, "Are you sure she wasn't playing possum?"

Longarm shook his head, disgusted with himself, as he replied, "Not hardly. I might have known they'd come back to remove the evidence. You check the mail poke whilst I see if they took the other bodies with 'em too."

They had. Neither the man he'd shot nor the one Calamity had put on the ground were anywhere about as he circled the crash site. He'd only had a quick look at the nondescript owlhoot Calamity had shot, but he'd sure been as dead as everyone else, for her Walker round had hit him in the head.

He walked back to the others, shaking his head as he said, "Well, not one of the three ever figure to bother us again, and it sure saves some digging for us honest folk."

The breed moved the buckboard around to the far side of the spilled coach as Calamity said, "Hot damn! I know why they done it. They knowed sooner or later you'd find out who ever'body *was*, right?"

"That's about the size of it, Calamity. I doubt the gal had any papers on her. They've been careful to use folks not too well covered by recent record. But she was too young to have spent much time in prison. All the guns they've pointed my way, so far, have been held by what I figure to be old convicts, just back in business and, lucky for me, a mite rusty."

Calamity wasn't listening. "Thunderation and shit!" she said. "How am I to prove I shot me a road agent if the rascal's body has been stole?"

"Don't see how you can. Who did you want to prove such a thing to, Calamity?"

"Them pesky reporters, of course. Sometimes I get the feeling folks don't take me *serious!* Ned Buntline writes about me right, but there's been a couple of mean-hearted reports that I'm a bullshitter. That stuck-up wife of old Jim told some reporters from back East that I was crazy to say her man was sweet on me."

Longarm could see she was building up a head of steam, so he said, "Yeah. Let's see about getting this coach back on its feet. Did they steal anything but the bodies?"

As she followed him around, she said, "Nope. The mail poke's still in the boot. Why do you ask?"

"Just making sure they was neither Indians nor road agents. Whoever's behind this spooky stuff is playing for higher stakes than the U.S. Mail."

The breed already had the block and tackle hooked to the luggage rails of the overturned Concord. Longarm nodded as he saw that the poles were wedged at the far end under the buckboard seat. He said, "I'll fetch a boulder whilst you lever her up a mite."

He moved away as the breed started hauling on the line, budging the Concord an inch at a time. He found a rock too heavy to lift but smooth enough to roll, so he started rolling it. By the time he got it over to the coach, there was space enough to roll it under and wedge it to hold the weight. He dusted off his hands and said, "Hand me that hook and I'll see if I can get it on the chassis."

The breed said to be careful, which hardly needed to be said to a man in Longarm's position as he got under the overhang on his hands and knees to get them a better purchase with the block and tackle. He crawled out, and the two of them hauled on the rope. That was all it took to crash the Concord upright on its wheels again. Calamity Jane threw her arms around him and gave him a big wet smack on the lips, saying, "Hot horse turds, I knowed I could count on you!"

He disengaged, red-faced, a mite surprised at how a critter that looked like an old hobo could kiss, as the breed tried not to laugh.

The breed moved the new team around to hitch it to the front as Longarm said, "Damn it, Calamity, you'll ruin my reputation if you don't mind your manners."

"I'll show you how to get ruint when we stop for the night at Pleasant Valley, honey bun."

He said, "No you won't. You see that extra mule I tied to the traces of the others?"

"I surely do. I meant to ask you why."

"Well, I'll tell you. I'm taking my McClellan and possibles, as well as myself, the rest of the way aboard that mule. The breed said it was all right."

"Thunderation and dogshit! Do you expect me to drive alone to Deadwood?"

"It won't be the first time, Calamity. I'd like to keep you company. But I'm in a hurry, and you may have noticed it ain't safe for gals to travel in my company. I'll make better time riding alone."

"Shoot, you'll look like a damn fool too, riding a *mule!*"

"I've done so before, and I ain't headed to Deadwood to be admired."

"Will you wait up for me at Pleasant Valley, honey bun? We both has to spend the infernal night someplace, and I sure admire you."

"I admire you too." He smiled gallantly, then he said, "I mean to push on through. Be interesting to hit Deadwood along about cock-crow, when me and anybody waiting up for me has the streets to ourselves. Look me up in Deadwood sometime, and I'll buy you a drink."

"Hot damn! Wait till they hear I drinks with Longarm as well as Jim Hickok!"

* * *

Mules were said to have more endurance than horses, which was about the only reason folks had for putting up with them. But the critter Longarm had saddled to ride must not have known he was a mule, and he obviously didn't want to be a saddle horse, either. So by the time they got that straightened out, along with one or two other problems, like getting lost in the dark, the sun rose to catch them still on the Deadwood trail, mad as hell at one another. So he had to ride into Deadwood by daylight, as the morning shift was heading for the mines.

Deadwood lay in Deadwood Gulch, which had been named in the Shining Times for the dead timber that was rafted down from the higher Black Hills to provide firewood and pit props to the first comers. The steep slopes all around were pitted with abandoned mineshafts; the gold rush of '76 had brought the usual pick-and-shovel fools, so a hell of a lot of sweat had gone into digging mica and fool's gold from the walls of the gulch. But some few had struck pay dirt, and so a town had mushroomed along the banks of Deadwood Creek. Deadwood was jerry-built, and hardly any of the false fronts facing the main street had been painted; the dry air and summer suns had silvered most of the wood by now. He noticed no new construction as he rode in.

He stopped first at the stage station to get rid of the ornery mule, and while he was at it, he tipped the Mexican stablehand a dime to let him leave his saddle and such there, for now. Then he went to wet his whistle before having breakfast and paying a few calls. He passed by the saloon where Hickok had been killed, since it was haunted, and charged too much anyway. The taps were open to serve the mining men, despite the hour. A couple of the Deadwood saloons, as well as all the whorehouses, were said to stay open all night. He went into the saloon near the railroad siding and was a mite surprised to find it so crowded this early in the morning. Some of the gents in there looked like they'd gotten a head start on him by drinking all night. He bellied up to the bar and asked for a schooner of beer. He wasn't out to get drunk with them; he just had a mortal thirst from all that dusty riding. He took a long healthy swig and figured he'd made the right move. Then he heard angry voices and wondered if he had.

He shot a casual glance behind him and saw that nobody was mad at him, but two gents facing one another across a card table in the corner were giving one another what-for.

They were both middle-aged, with drinker's noses. It was up for grabs who was wearing the funnier outfit. One had on a hat big enough for a family of Lakota to live in and, not content with that, wore a buckskin shirt all prissied up with beadwork and fringes long enough to trip over.

The man across from him sported a Louis Napoleon beard and mustache, and wore his hat pancaked, with a rattlesnake hatband. His clothes would have looked more sensible on a Mexican vaquero with a taste for black leather and German silver conchos. As Longarm stared at them, bemused, the one in black shouted, "You're a damned liar! I was here first, and I am the one and only!"

Big Hat rose, exposing a brace of ivory-gripped, silver-mounted sixguns as he yelled, red-faced, "Nobody calls me a liar and lives, you son of a bitch!"

Longarm saw that everyone else in the place was getting out of range, so he moved down to the far end of the bar, holding his beer in his left hand in case he suddenly needed to use his right. He figured he might when the one in black got up, yelling, "Fill your fists, you rascal!" and they both went for their guns.

It was one of the longest gunfights Longarm had ever seen. They both packed two guns, and by the time they'd fired off a score of rounds at one another at point-blank range, there was so much smoke he couldn't see who'd won. He put his beer on the bar and drew his own .44, just in case, as the blue haze slowly cleared.

with the resources to get it out."

"You mean with expensive chemistry and moving a lot of ore?"

"Yeah. The highgrade's gone, along with most of the gut-and-git small mining outfits. Some Eastern syndicates has been buying up and consolidating the claims to work the rock more scientific-like."

He took a sip of beer before he added, "In a way, it'll make for some peaceable changes in these parts. Miners working for day wages don't shoot up the place as much of a Saturday night. They've built a schoolhouse and a couple of churches, and when the Dakotas become states, we mean to be the county seat. We aim to call it Lawrence County. Ain't that a bitch?"

Longarm stared down at his nearly empty schooner as he mused, "Might be, to the folks down the draw at that other town called Lead. Have they been disputing your claims to county seathood?"

"Naw, why should they? There ain't hardly anything in Lead but that one mine. Deadwood's the only important camp worth mention in these parts. Why do you ask?"

"Well, to get to be the county seat, a town's got to publish some imposing population figures, and somebody don't want Washington to know for certain how many head of folks there are in these parts."

"I follow your drift. But like I said, Lead is only a wide spot in the road and there must be, oh, a couple of thousand folks here in Deadwood, counting women and children."

"But nobody knows for certain, right? You could lose a couple hundred votes easy in a rough estimate like that, and a couple hundred votes could swing an election."

"Hell, Long, we don't vote for the territorial government yet. Washington appoints it."

"I know. But you do get to vote in national elections. And if the territory ever means to be a state, you'll need to have the population to qualify. How many folks would you say there might be dwelling in the Dakotas at the moment?"

"White folks? Beats hell out of me. You might have noticed, towns and homesteads is spread out thin in these parts. Are you saying some rascal's clouding the figures to keep us from statehood?"

"Don't know. Maybe somebody don't want statehood, or maybe it's the other way around and they mean to get her by padding the figures. If I knew which, I'd be closer to some answers."

The town law looked puzzled. "I don't see how it matters all that much, either way, to most folk. Like you said, we get most all our constitutional rights, whether we're a state or a territory."

"You're right," Longarm said. "It don't affect most folks all that much. But the rascals trying to keep us from holding a census ain't most folks. They're *hiding* something."

He rose to his feet and extended his hand to the local lawman. "It's been nice jawing with you. But I'd best see if there's any Western Union answers to some wires I sent last night."

There were. The Census Bureau had sent him a night letter informing him there was nobody named Charity Kirby working out of the Denver office and that, of course, they hadn't assigned anyone from there to the Dakota crew. The information was a mite late to do him—or Charity—much good, but it was nice to see he'd guessed right about that egret hat.

The misnamed Palace Hotel was a ramschackle structure with a wraparound veranda and mighty crude plumbing, even for the Dakotas. But they'd managed some potted palms for the lobby. He wondered how the little trees survived in such dim light. He told the desk clerk who he was looking for and said he might as well hire a room there while he was at it, since he'd be working with the census takers upstairs. The room clerk gave him a key and sent the bellhop up to fetch somebody from the census crew, while Longarm took a seat under a palm. That was when he noticed it was a fake, made out of wire and waxed silk. The buffalo head over the desk looked real, though.

He lit one of the cigars he'd taken off the dead bushwhacker, and had it going good when the bellhop led a couple of folks down the stairs. One was a man in a checkered suit, and the other was a blonde gal he'd seen somewhere before but couldn't place.

She wasn't bad looking, in a tired sort of way; he knew he'd never kissed her, and he'd remember her if he'd seen her face on a reward poster. The gent in the checkered suit was a stranger to him too, until he introduced himself as Howard Redfern and said the gal was his wife, Penny. Longarm figured that had to stand for Penelope, for she didn't look like a penny at all. She looked worn and faded, despite being fairly well shaped, and she had decent features. Maybe the thin air out here in the high country was giving her a hard time.

They all sat down, and Redfern said he had a crew of eight in and about the hotel. He added that they were raring to go, saying, "I don't understand our orders, Deputy. We can't get any facts and figures, just sitting here in town."

Longarm nodded soothingly and said, "I know. But before we spread a corporal's squad of census takers out in the great unknown, I'd like to get a better handle on what happened to the ones who went out to ask questions and never came back. Were you here in town at the time?"

"No. I've been here a few days, and Penny here just joined me. I don't know why they got rid of those others. The figures they had jibe with mine."

"You and your crew have been taking a census?"

"Just here in Deadwood, as we were waiting for you. The last bunch counted a little over two thousand here in the town proper. I have the exact figures in my briefcase, upstairs, if you need them."

Longarm shook his head and said, "No, thanks. Counting

heads is *your* job. You say the last crew counted the same. How about all that other stuff you ask, about race, religion, bathtubs and such?"

Redfern nodded and said, "Our two tallies agree almost exactly."

"Almost?"

"Well, you have to understand that people move in and out of town on a day-to-day basis. We're after averages, not Holy Writ engraved in stone. There were no changes in voter registration, save for one Republican who seems to have died last week, and he was seventy-eight, in case that worries you."

Longarm laughed and said, "Don't worry me as much as it must have bothered that old Repulican. I'll take your word that the folks here in the town ain't bashful about being counted by the census. Nobody seems to have bothered any of you, here in Deadwood. So whatever it is they're trying to hide must be out of town a ways."

"That's obvious," Redfern said. "And I don't see how we're going to find out what it might be, just sitting here."

Longarm snubbed out the cigar, since the pale gal sitting quietly by was looking sort of pained. He said, "I'd best scout a mite. Why don't you give me one of those books you write things down in, and I'll ride out and see if anybody aims to shoot me for asking."

Redfern looked at him dubiously. "You're not a census taker."

"I know. But I can read and write, and I've sure *answered* enough of the fool questions. My figures don't have to go down official, if you're worried about me horning in. It won't matter if I get some facts and figures wrong. I just want to see how willing folks in these parts are to answer them, and if they ain't, why not."

Redfern shrugged and turned to his wife. "Penny, go up to our room and fetch some blank forms for the deputy." It was like he was ordering a stablehand. The blonde flinched as though she'd been slapped, but rose without a word. Longarm didn't say anything. It wasn't his woman who'd been spoken to in that tone, which was lucky for Redfern. The dude must have read some distaste in Longarm's eye; he smiled and said, "If you must know, we haven't been getting along too well of late."

Longarm said, "That's between you and the lady. This thin air makes some folks edgy."

"Oh, we're not from the East. Our home's in Wyoming now. We've been out here a couple of years. When I'm not taking the census I work for Interior, in Casper."

Longarm remembered where he'd seen the dishwater blonde before. He only hoped she didn't remember him. He knew it was a small world, but this was ridiculous.

The fresh little kid he'd last seen on the train came down with a sheaf of papers and said, "Mama said to give you these, Mr. Redfern. She's laying down, feeling poorly again."

Then, as Redfern took the census forms from him, the kid looked up at Longarm and said, "How do? Ain't you the cowboy that was rasslin' with the lady on the train?"

Longarm shook his head and said, "I arrived aboard a mule, sonny. I disremember rasslin' anybody else."

Redfern said, "That will be all, David Boggs. Why don't you go outside and look for snakes or something."

The sarcasm was lost on the kid, who shouted, "Oh, boy, snakes!" and ran out of the lobby.

Redfern handed the papers to Longarm and said, "We can spare these, I suppose. That was my stepson, by the way."

"I figured he might be, having a different name and all."

Redfern repressed a grimace of distaste as he said, "She wanted me to give him my name. But that'll be the day. The damned brat gets on my nerves."

"I can see he's sort of imaginative. Didn't you know the lady had the kid when you married up with her?"

"I wasn't paying attention, I guess. You know how it is when you want a woman and she holds out for a damned old ring."

Longarm nodded but didn't answer. It seemed impolite to say that whenever he ran into that particular problem, it seemed more sensible to just let the gal go. He could see that Redfern was one of those hard-driving types who hated to take no for an answer. Longarm didn't like such answers much, either, but he tended to think ahead. A man had no call marrying up with a gal if he didn't think he'd want her as much after the honeymoon was over.

To cover his feelings, Longarm started leafing through the census forms and carbon-papered instruction sheets in his lap. But he must have been frowning because Redfern asked, "What's the matter, words too big for you?"

That was uncivil enough for Longarm to frown right at him as he replied, "I savvy more big words than you might think, friend. I've never seen much use in saying 'render unto me the sodium chloride,' when 'pass the salt' would do as well and likely get quicker results. But I get to read lots of fancy words in my line of work. Meet a lot of fancy dudes, too. Ain't got much use for neither."

Redfern looked away as he saw he'd met his match in veiled sarcasm, and to ease out of a collision course he said, "I suppose you do serve a lot of papers written in legalese. You'll want to meet the others before you leave, won't you?"

Longarm shook his head and said, "No point in that, till I see how much of a herding job I have. I'll meet up with everybody at suppertime, here in the hotel dining room. Meanwhile, I'll make a run down toward Lead. It's only three or four miles each way."

Redfern frowned and protested, "That means another day of just sitting here doing nothing, damn it!"

Longarm said, "I know. But you're getting paid by the day, and you must not have been listening. I said I was taking the trail down to the next camp, at Lead."

"So?"

"So the last two census takers that vanished from human ken did so on the trail from Deadwood to Lead. That's why I'm heading down that way alone, and why I don't want anybody else to try her until I find out why the U.S. Census is so unpopular in that direction."

Chapter 8

Longarm swung his hired chestnut mare off the main wagon trace following the north-south rail line when he spied the cabin up the slope, half hidden by second-growth aspen. As he approached, a gent who really looked like Rip Van Winkle came out on the porch with an old Henry rifle. He was maybe a hundred years old, give or take a dozen, and his long white beard was as dirty as the rest of him. As Longarm rode within shouting range, the old-timer shouted, "Get thee gone, goddammit! This here's private property, you claim-jumping rascal!"

Longarm dismounted on the far side as he said, "I ain't after your gold, I'm after your vital statistics. I'm taking a census for the U.S. government, and I aim to ask you some questions."

"Go to hell and take the infernal government with you!

Like I tolt them other fellers, who I be and what I be doing here ain't none of your goddam beeswax! You got about ten seconds to git offen my claim, young feller. I warns you, I'm ornery as hell, and this Henry's *loaded!*"

Longarm knew now that the others had gotten this far, if the old coot hadn't shot them and tossed them down that mine shaft up the slope. He came around the chestnut's rump, keeping his own gun hand polite as he smiled and said, "I can see you're not a man to trifle with, sir. So we don't have to go inside and I don't want to look under your beard. I just have some questions to ask you."

"I don't want to answer no questions. I ain't done nothing unlawful, and if anybody says I have, let 'em come forward with a warrant fer my arrest."

Longarm reached in his shirt for two smokes, and held one out to the hermit as he said, "I'll tell you true that a man can get arrested for refusing to answer the census. It hardly seems fair to me, neither. But that's the law, and it's federal."

The old man ignored the offer. So Longarm lit his own as the hermit protested, "That's downright unconstituted! The law has no call to pester folks as hasn't done nothing to nobody!"

Longarm shook out his match, broke the stem, and, because he was on another man's property, put the spent match in his pocket as he said, "I fear it's in the Constitution that a census is to be held every ten years, sir. I know it's a bother, but the Founding Fathers put it in, so what are we going to do about it?"

"That's crazy. Jefferson and them other gents was for free and easy ways. Why would they put a dumb thing like that in the Bill of Rights?"

"It ain't in the Bill of Rights. It's in the fine print. As to why they done it, it only stands to reason that for a democratic form of government to work, you gotta know who in hell is out there voting for you. The Lower House is seated in proportion to the population in each congress-man's district, which is only fair, and how in thunder can they do that if they don't know whether he's voting for folks or tree stumps?"

He took out the form he'd brought from his saddlebag, and put the refused cigar back in his shirt pocket to replace it with a pencil stub as he added, "I'm counting one head here. You live alone?"

"Hell, no, can't you see my harem of dancing gals? 'Course I lives alone, goddamn your eyes! I've learned the hard way that women ain't no good and I've never fancied screwing men."

Longarm looked around and said, "I can't write that down on this loose paper. Let's set on the porch so's I can lay the form on the planking."

Then he stepped around the old man and his old gun without waiting for an answer. The hermit followed him to the porch, complaining, "You stay out here, savvy? I don't allow nobody but my dog inside my cabin, and I don't allow Old Blue inside unless it's raining fire and salt!"

Longarm eased himself down on the porch, propping his boot heels in the dooryard dust as he spread the forms on the rough pine. The old man hooked a boot up on the porch and grounded the rifle, but he muttered something awful about Longarm's mother as he did so.

Longarm said, "I could put you down as a John Doe, if you ain't aiming to vote this November."

"Who says I can't vote? I aims to vote for Garfield, dammit!"

"That's your privilege. But I'd best put your right name down to avoid confusion at the ballot box."

The hermit hesitated, then said, "All right, my handle is Pete Culhane, and that's all I aims to tell you and it'll cost you that smoke!"

Longarm handed up the cigar he'd taken off the dead outlaw and said, "That sounds reasonable, Mr. Culhane. I can fill in most of the other squares. I can see you ain't a Christian, so I'll just put down 'atheist' where it asks your creed."

"Hold on, you know-it-all rascal! I'll have you know I'm as good a Christian as *you* might be! You see *me* roaming about the country pestering folks as ain't done me no harm? I may not go to church regular. But that gives you no call to call me no infernal atheist!"

"I stand corrected. Culhane's an Irish name, so you're likely Roman Catholic, right?"

"Wrong, goddamn your eyes! My people come from Ulster and I was birthed a decent Presbyterian. So you ain't as smart as you thought you was after all."

"I reckon you got me on that one, pard. Let's see now, we both know you're a white man and I can tell from your accent that you was raised on this side of the water, so we can likely put you down as a naturalized citizen of foreign birth, right?"

"Wrong again, by jimmies! I was bred and birthed in Dade County, Georgia!"

Longarm grinned sheepishly up at the old man as the hermit lit the cigar with a smug expression. He said, "This just ain't my day, I reckon. But if you're a Georgia boy, it's safe to assume you're a reconstructed Reb who fought for the South."

"Well, hell, of *course* I fit for the South, you dumb cuss! Would you expect a Georgia boy to be riding for the *North*? I fit at Cold Harbor and took me a minny ball in the leg at Chickamauga. But we won at Chickamauga, dammit!"

"So I hear tell. You're a mite long in the tooth to have been a private, no offense, so I'm putting down that you was an officer."

"Well, I was only a staff sergeant, but you can say I was a officer if you like. Did you ride in the War, son?"

"Yeah, I disremember which side. I reckon we'd best put this spread down as a livestock operation, I can see you have no standing crops. What do you raise here, cows or sheep?"

"Cows or sheep? Did your mother drop you on your head a lot as a child? Anyone can see it's a mining claim! I ain't no infernal stockman!"

Longarm made the notation. He knew better than to ask a grown man what he made a year. That was why that British income tax that some fool in Washington was jawing about would never come to pass while American men still stood up to piss. Anyone could see it was downright indecent to ask a man how much money he made. He told the old-timer, "I know this is dumb, but they want to know if you have one of them new telephone sets."

The old man choked on his smoke, slapped his knee, and said, "That's a good one. What else do they want to know? I'll confess right out I don't own a hot-air balloon, and I lent my locomotive to the neighbors. But I've seen one of them new Edison lamps. Are you putting that down?"

"Can't. Not unless you got your cabin wired for such."

"Jesus H. Christ, do they ask questions like *that,* too?"

"Yep. I can't see why, neither. Look here, where it asks if you have running water or inside plumbing. Seems to me that Congress ought to be able to get by, just knowing you're here. It ain't no business of their'n whether you get your water from yon pump and shit out back like everybody else, right?"

"Damn right, son. But you may as well put me down for a civilized two-holer, as long as they ask. I wouldn't want folks in Washington to think I squat in the brush like a damned old Sioux!"

Longarm grinned as he finished filling in the personal questions on sanitary facilities, and didn't bother to ask as he checked off the squares asking about school-age children of the household and whether they went to public or private schools. The old man sat down beside him, leaning the rifle on the porch steps as he enjoyed the smoke and company more. He said, "I suspicion by the twang in your dulcet tones that you hail from the hill country, same as me. Where'd you say you was from?"

Longarm smiled and said, "Sorry. Forgot my manners. My name is Custis Long, and I first saw the light in West-by-God-Virginia."

"We had us a boy named Long in the Georgia Militia. Got kilt at Shiloh."

Longarm had been under fire at Shiloh too, but he didn't say so. It was a long time ago, and old war stories tended to be old *bore* stories if you didn't nip 'em in the bud. So he just nodded and said, "Well, I see we have most of these infernal questions answered, and 'fess up, it didn't hurt as much as going to the dentist, did it?"

"Well, you ask questions more polite than them other jaspers. I run 'em off with Old Betsy here. But you can stay and have your noon dinner with me if you like, if you promise not to write down what I eats for dinner."

Longarm glanced up at the sun and said, "I'd admire that, Mr. Culhane, but I've some riding to do before noon. I'd be proud to set a spell and jaw, though. You say those other census takers rode on from here?"

"Yep, down towards Lead. Sheriff says they never come back. Ain't that a bitch? To tell the truth, that's one reason I might have seemed a mite testy when we first met up, Mr. Long. That fool sheriff pestered hell outten me about them census boys. They even insisted on searching my grounds, and poked about under my cabin. Worse yet, they made me show them through my mine, and it made me mad as hell!"

Longarm gazed at the black square of the one-man adit up the slope as he digested the fact that he didn't have to come up with a graceful way of searching it after all. The old man took a drag on his smoke and added, "I watched the sheriff and his deputies as they was poking about my claim, but I'll vow they highgraded a couple of ore samples anyhow. You know who I think put 'em up to it? Them rascals at the Homestake Mine in Lead, that's who!"

Longarm frowned and asked, "Why would the operators of the Homestake want to vanish census takers, Mr. Culhane?"

"Hell, son, I never said they done nothing to no census takers. I meant they put the sheriff up to accusing me, so's they could have a look down my shaft and report to that infernal Hearst feller!"

"Does old Senator Hearst own the Homestake diggings in Lead?"

"Not right out. He's just one of the stockholders. But they say he's ornery as hell, and the syndicate's been trying to buy out all us little fellers in the gulch."

"So I heard. But I brushed with the Hearst mining outfit out California way a little while ago, and they turned out not guilty. Old George Hearst ain't no sissy. You don't get to be a mining magnate and a senator besides by feeding stray cats and doing favors for the folks down the road. But I can't see old George Hearst as an outright murderer."

"You wasn't listening, boy. I never said the folks at the Homestake *kilt* them census takers. I said they took advantage of it to pressure me."

"Are you worth pressuring?"

"Wait here. I got something to show you."

So Longarm folded the census forms away and stayed put as the old man took his rifle in the cabin and came out with a rock about the size of his fist. He hunkered down by Longarm, handed him the sample, and said, "You tell me, if you're so smart."

Longarm held the hunk of quartz up to the light as he peered at it from all sides before he said, "I don't see much color, Mister Culhane."

"Shoot, I thought you sounded smarter than that. The gut-and-gitters got all the flake and wire gold out long ago. That's bread-and-butter ore."

"You mean low grade?"

"It ain't *that* low a grade, dammit! It's true you got to use a little cyanide and a lot of sweat to get the color outten ore like that, but I got me a whole infernal mountain of the stuff behind me, and by jimmies, it's all *mine!* I ain't selling out to them fancy dudes over to Lead!"

Longarm said he wouldn't, either, as he got to his feet, thanked the old-timer for his time, and forked himself back on the chestnut. He could see how taking a census in these parts was figuring to be slow work, if half the others were as hard to get to know.

He'd have to give the census takers some advice on handling folks out here. Meanwhile, he'd traced the missing men this far at least, and what the old man had said about mining claims was sort of interesting; he meant to dig deeper into the matter. But at the moment he couldn't see how the gold of the Black Hills tied in with someone trying to prevent a census. The whole world knew there was gold in these here hills. The Sioux War of '76 had been fought over the damned gold, despite all the bullshit about sacred Indian hunting grounds. The Pine Ridge tribal leaders were still trying to sue Washington for the six million dollars they'd been promised for the Black Hills and never gotten. Meanwhile, they even wrote fool stories over in London, England, about the desperate doings of Deadwood Dick in the gold fields here. The Homestake was said to be one of the richest gold mines on earth. They weren't trying to hide it; they were selling stock like mad to pay for the expensive gear it took to win color from their vast but low-grade holdings. There was nothing about gold mining in the infernal census forms anyway.

He asked his mount, "Do you reckon somebody means to hide the number of hard-rock miners working in these parts? Someone playing a Wall Street shell game might not want a head count. You can halfway judge how well gold futures might be doing, if you know for sure how many folks are digging the stuff."

103

The mare didn't answer, so he shook his head and said, "Hold on. That won't work. The miners has a union. So the numbers are a matter of public record. Redfern already told us the miners back in Deadwood didn't raise a fuss about being counted."

He'd about finished his smoke, so he snubbed it out on a passing tree and made sure it was out before he got rid of it, muttering, "The old man's notion that someone's using skull duggery to jump his claim won't work neither. In all modesty, any gang who was willing to tangle with me and Calamity Jane could have one old man living alone for breakfast. The Homestake syndicate might want his mountain, but not bad enough to kill for it, or they'd have already done so."

He would have missed the cabin on the other side of the gulch if he hadn't spotted its smoke above the aspen crowns. The missing census takers, being greenhorns, might not have spotted it at all. But just in case they had, he decided to check it out.

The mysterious cabin lay in a clearing, guarded by a dog—on a chain, fortunately—that looked half wolf and howled like he was trying to prove it. But he got a more friendly reception from the two gals who came out on the porch to see what the hound was baying at. One of them yelled at the dog to hush. So he did, which was just as well, because Longarm's mare was getting spooked. He patted her neck to steady her as he swung out of the saddle and tethered her to an aspen. One of the gals came out to greet him, in her bare feet and a thin smock made of flour sacking that didn't hide much. She was a strawberry blonde with big, dumb, baby-blue eyes. Except for looking sort of stupid, she was pretty enough and her figure was downright inspiring. "Howdy," she said. "If you're selling anything, forget it. We're too poor to buy a sewing machine or a set of encyclopedias. Be careful what you say in front of my kid sister, yonder on the porch. She's tetched in the head."

Longarm shook the hand she held out like a man, noting that while her smaller paw was callused, it sure didn't feel like shaking hands with a man. He said, "Howdy. My name's Custis Long and I'm taking census for the government."

"Well, I'm Rosemary Dill and my sister's name is Lavender and we don't have no census to give you, but if there's anything else we can do for you, let us know."

He grinned and said, "You don't understand, Miss Rosemary. The U.S. Census is a head count of the U.S. citizens living in the country right now. Can I take it nobody else from the Census Bureau has been by to talk with you ladies?"

"Nope. Hardly anybody ever comes by here, consarn it. We raise eggs for the folks in town each ways. Chickens is piss-poor company. The reason I'm dressed like this is 'cause I was just fixing to clean the coops out back. But they can wait. Come over to the house and tell us about this here census critter."

So he went. The other one ran inside as they approached, but not before he'd noticed that she was built just as impressively and was even prettier, with her hair a darker shade that almost matched the rump of his hired mount. Rosemary led him inside. The cabin was clean, if sparely furnished, with planks and box shelves, a couple of nail kegs for sitting around the plank table, and one big brass bedstead in the corner. Lavender Dill was up on the bedstead with her knees doubled under her, looking at him with scared eyes and blushing like a rose. Her older sister said, "Pay her no mind. She ain't used to men folk. Set yourself down whilst I cake and coffee you some."

He took a seat on the keg, placing his hat on the table and spreading the census forms out on the pine table while she rustled them up refreshments.

She plunked down two tin cups of Arbuckle and two tin plates of chocolate cake.

"What about the other lady?" Longarm asked.

The strawberry blonde said, "Lavender ain't a lady. She's a lunatic. The doc in town says she's a nymphomorph or something like that."

"Uh, nymphomaniac?" he asked nervously.

"Yeah, that sounds more like it. Whatever she is, I have to watch her or she does scandalous things to that dog outside. Don't that sound crazy to you?"

"Uh, I'm not a doctor. This cake sure tastes fine, Miss Rosemary. But can we get to the census? I'm supposed to fill in these blanks for you, see?"

"You'll have to. I don't know how to write. What's your pleasure?"

So Longarm started asking and she started answering and it went smoothly, since they didn't have much to answer to the government for. The two gals had been orphaned a couple of years by the cholera carrying off their elders. They had no assets to report but this quarter-section claim, and he took her word that they had enough chickens out back to keep them going, with eggs selling for two bits apiece in the mining area. The cabin was a one-roomer, so he filled in the part about them using an outhouse without asking a lady such questions. He'd already seen the water pump out front. She said her late father had been a registered Democrat, but of course, being females, neither of them got to vote, even if the one on the bed had been right in the head. Rosemary was twenty-two and Lavender was nineteen, making them both lawful to kiss, but he decided not to think about that. He had some riding to do, and his old organ-grinder had no call to tingle in his britches like that just because a half-undressed gal was sitting next to him batting her eyelashes as she answered his fool questions. She couldn't read, but she could see he was getting near the end of the form, so she said, "You sure do ask a lot of fool questions. Let me ask you a couple. Are you married?"

"Not hardly. I move about too much. So I ain't fixing to get hitched in the near future, neither."

"I ain't sure I'm ready to settle down with one gent, yet. Do you like girls?"

"Sure I do. Doesn't every man?"

She laughed and said, "Not our two nearest neighbors, at your next stop. They're calt Bruce and Billy and when they moved in to run cows in the aspen I figured it was our lucky day, for they're both right nice-looking boys. But I wasted a mess of coffee and cake afore I found out they was even crazier than Lavender over there, and— Dammit, Lavender, stop doing that in front of company!"

Longarm resisted the impulse to glance over his shoulder to see exactly what Lavender was supposed to stop doing.

Rosemary said, "The doc in town thinks it's the altitude out here what makes folks so randy. Bruce and Billy are randy as hell, but only for each other. I come across 'em in the aspen one evening. They couldn't even wait to get back to their cabin and close the blinds. Boy, they sure was going at it hot and heavy."

Longarm cleared his throat loudly. "Can we get on with these last few questions, Miss Rosemary?"

So she behaved herself until he'd finished her form and put it away. Then she said, "I've studied on me and old Lavender pleasuring each other. Lord knows it's lonesome out here in the aspen. But that'd be queer, wouldn't it?"

"Yeah. It might be considered incest too, in a way. I ain't sure on the statutes when it comes to a brother or sister of the same sex, but common sense says that if brother and sister is incest, sister and sister ought to be."

Longarm found the exchange distasteful and embarrassing, and it was giving him a hard-on besides, so he said, "I'd best be on my way, Miss Rosemary. I thank you for the coffee and cake and your wholehearted cooperation with the federal government."

But as he rose, she got up too, and put her arms around him, saying, "Hold on, I pleasured you. Don't you aim to stay a spell and pleasure us?"

"*Us?* You're getting me all flustered, Miss Rosemary."

"Yeah, I didn't think that was a gun you was aiming at me down there."

"He's pretty," Lavender offered from the corner.

Longarm said, "I'd be a liar if I denied that your offer tempted me, Miss Rosemary. But I'm on duty and, uh, I ain't sure a census taker's supposed to get so personal."

"Kill him if he tries to leave," suggested Lavender, adding, "Get Daddy's gun and shoot him down. He's a sissy, like them others!"

He laughed and said, "Well, I would be a sissy if a lady had to pull a gun on me to get me to kiss her."

So he kissed her. She flattened her thinly clad body against his and kissed back wildly as the sister on the bed started bobbing up and down, crying out, "Oh, he's staying, he's staying, and we're gonna have some fun!"

They did, too. By the time Longarm had his duds off, the two gals were waiting naked atop the quilted bedspread. It was high morning, and the sunlight through the bottle-glass windows didn't hide a hair on their young and eager bodies. They were both clean looking, except for some dirt on the soles of their feet, and as he climbed in bed with them he wished he'd been born with two of *everything*, since no matter who he started with, the other was just as desirable.

By the time all three had finished coming, they were in a tangled knot on the bed and he was nibbling one of Lavender's nipples as one or the other of them was kneading his half-soft and rather abused virile member with slightly less enthusiasm.

He said, "Ladies, this has got past pleasure into pure bragging. I have to move it down the road."

Rosemary laughed and said, "If we let you up, can we count on you coming this way again?"

"Honey, if there was another way to come, we must have missed it. I'll likely stop by again, being only human. But

I got a job to do, and while I'd be a dirty dog to suggest that my time here had been wasted, there's only so many hours in a day, and this one's starting to wear a mite thin."

So they both kissed him all over, and sat on either side, still naked, as he regretfully hauled on his duds and boots. He didn't suspect them of waylaying the missing census takers. He could see that they were too friendly to use any weapons on a man but the dangerously eager bodies with which the Lord in his infinite wisdom, and likely in a moment of humor, had endowed them.

The room sort of swayed as he got to his feet to strap on his gun rig. He figured it was likely the strong coffee, and by the time he'd kissed them both, noting how much more naked a gal's bare flesh felt against rough wool, he'd recovered his balance and was able to walk out to the tethered mare without staggering.

Chapter 9

"Go away!" called the kid on the porch of the next spread he rode into, as Longarm and the mare kept coming. The kid on the porch yelled, "I warn you!" in a high voice.

Longarm saw that he wasn't pointing anything serious at him. So he got down, soberly tethered the mare to the rail of the porch, and said, "Howdy, I'm Custis Long and I'm taking the U.S. Census, come hell or high water. Is your, ah, sidekick about?"

"Bruce is out looking for strays. He'll hurt you if he comes back to find you trifling with me."

"I ain't here to trifle with you, ah, sir. You must have heard this is a census year. So I have to ask you some questions."

"Go away. We don't have to answer anything. We haven't done anything to harm anyone."

"Nobody says you have, friend. Before I take down your vital statistics, did a couple of other gents from the Census Bureau drop by a few days ago?"

"One of them did. Bruce chased him off our property. This is posted property, mister. Didn't you read that sign down by the wagon trace?"

"I did. It said 'No Trespassing.' But I ain't a trespasser. I'm a federal agent, and like I said, you got to cooperate with your old Uncle Sam."

He joined the sissified-looking little jasper on the porch, as the latter edged away nervously. Longarm sat down and spread the papers, as he had at Pete Culhane's, and said, "I can fill in most of the lines since I'm getting good at guessing about plumbing fixtures and such in the Dakota Territories. But you're supposed to tell me the names of everybody living here. Naturally, you don't have any kids, right?"

"Not yet," said the one who had to be Billy. He sounded like he meant it. Longarm felt too sorry for him to grin. Some men seemed to feel a need to persecute Billy's kind, but Longarm was a live-and-let-live sort of fellow who had no doubts about himself, so he couldn't understand mistreating men that nature had dealt a different hand. He had no idea what made some men that way, but since he was a lawman and not a sawbones, he didn't think it was any of his business. So his voice was pleasant as he said, "I got to get some last names down. If you ain't Bruce, you must be Billy, right?"

"Yes. Billy Murdstone. Who told you about us, those dreadful Dill sisters? What did they tell you about Bruce and me?"

"Just your names," he lied, adding, "I was just at their place, asking the same questions."

"I'll bet. Did they tell you what sluts they were?"

"Mr. Murdstone, it ain't the job of the U.S. Census to spread neighborhood gossip. Everything I hear is treated

111

confidential, and nobody this side of Washington gets to look at such answers as I put on this paper. Do we have us a deal?"

"We'd best wait until my husband gets back."

"Uh, look, there's nothing in this questionnaire covering such matters. Your personal relations with the other gent here are your own business. What's his last name, by the way?"

"Murdstone, of course. I took his name when I married him."

Longarm shot the kid an annoyed look. Billy Murdstone was maybe five foot nine and built skinny and weak looking. He wore his sandy hair long for a he and short for a she. He was a tolerable-looking little cuss, if you admired a weak jawline and big soft eyes on a man. Longarm didn't. He said, "Look, kid, I'm trying to be polite. But let's cut this bullshit. You are what you are and we'll say no more about it. But I can't hardly put down two men in the U.S. Census as man and wife. If you and your, uh, sidekick want to use the same last name, it's no never-mind to me. I'll just put you down as the Murdstone boys and let 'em think you're brothers or something."

Before Billy could answer, a burlier-looking man rode into the dooryard on a black bronc that matched his hair and whiskers. He roared out, "What's going on here?" so Longarm got to his feet. This fellow didn't look sissy at all, and he was wearing a mighty masculine S&W .44 on his hip.

As he dismounted, the one called Billy shouted, "It's all right, dear heart. He's from the Census Bureau, like that other man."

Bruce dismounted and came over, scowling, to say, "I warned you all to stay away from me and mine." Then he turned to Billy to ask, "Has he been trifling with you, honey?"

"No, dear," Billy said. "He's been a perfect gentleman, and I fear we must cooperate. He's explained that it's federal regulations, and they'll just keep sending people until we do."

Bruce shook his head and said, "Damn it, Billy, we can't! It'll all come out about you and me."

Longarm said, "Before you cloud up and rain all over me, the way you boys has been carrying on up here ain't exactly a neighborhood secret. As I was just telling your young pal here, everything you tell me is confidential by law in the first place, and Washington ain't all that interested in what you do in your spare time."

Bruce hesitated, and Billy said, "I'm afraid he already knows, dear. I told you Rosemary Dill saw us that time in the aspen, remember?" Billy blushed and added, "We shouldn't have let ourselves get carried away like that, but I'm not ashamed."

Bruce looked at Longarm and asked, "What's the penalty for lying to the U.S. Census?"

"Same as refusing to cooperate. You can be fined or sent to jail either way. So what's it going to be? I told you I don't mean to put nothing down about you boys being fond of one another."

Bruce sighed and said, "You're going to have to, if the report on us is to read true. You're sure nobody out here will ever see it?"

"Honest Injun. I could go to jail, myself, for revealing any census records."

Bruce nodded and said, "All right. Put Billy down as my wife. Common-law wife, anyways. And spell her name B-I-L-L-I-E."

"Like a gal's?"

"She *is* a gal, damn it. What do you take me for, a *queer?*"

Longarm stared at him, puzzled, and said, "If you ain't, you sure have gone to a heap of trouble convincing the whole territory. You'd better go back to the beginning and explain a few things to me, friend."

Bruce Murdstone said, "There's not that much to explain. You see, we're Mormons. Or we used to be. The Elders had chosen Billie to be the bride of another, but she was in love with me and I was in love with her, so we ran away together."

Longarm shot a suspicious look at Billy, or Billie, and he—or she—nodded and pulled the loose hickory shirt closer, so he could see the outline of the little cupcakes under it. She had mighty small tits for a female, but he'd never seen any at all on a male, so he said, "I don't need to examine nobody. But what the hell makes you want to convince everybody that you're a couple of gents? I know some Latter-Day Saints, and while they seem a mite strict about drinking coffee and dipping snuff, that Avenging Angel stuff stopped about the time Brother Brigham died a spell ago."

Bruce Murdstone said, "A lot you know! It's true the Salt Lake Temple is run these days by responsible men and doesn't do anything but expel Saints who break the faith. But Billie and me didn't run away from Salt Lake. We're from a community that still clings to the old ways. They aimed to marry Billie to an Elder who already had four wives, and there were Avenging Angels enough after us as we lit out! I don't think you understand how seriously the older Mormons take breaking the faith, Mr. Long."

Longarm grimaced and said, "You're wrong. Some Avenging Angels left me stranded to die in the Great Salt Desert one time. I put that bunch out of business, and the army hanged the bunch that wiped out the wagon train at Mountain Meadows and blamed it on the Utes. But I follow your drift, and I can see why you'd rather have folks call you a sissy than the husband of a runaway Mormon bride-to-be."

He thought and then added, "Living a lie is awesomely complicated. If Billie here ever gets in a family way, it figures to get even more so. Can you imagine the talk in these parts if the doc had to pay a birthing call on a house inhabited by sissies?"

"We've, ah, been careful."

"Yeah, but sooner or later you'll be wanting kids anyway. It's only natural. So let me ask you something. Are you two still practicing Mormons?"

"We live by *The Book of Mormon* and the revelations of Joseph Smith, if that's what you mean."

"That's what I meant. The price of beef is up this summer, and the big mining outfits are buying all the land for sale within miles. So the first thing you two ought to do is sell out while the selling's good."

"We've already had fair offers," Bruce said. "But where could we go that the Avenging Angels wouldn't be likely to find us?"

"The last place they'd look, of course. Mormons stand out in these parts, even when they don't look queer. But a Mormon couple in Salt Lake City would stand out about as much as an A-rab couple in Mecca. I told you I'd brushed with some fanatics calling themselves Saints before. They don't spend much time in Salt Lake. The *real* Elders of the Church don't think much of 'em, and the Salt Lake coppers frown on gun-toting, as well as on tobacco and coffee. You two would be safer there among your own kind than any other place I can come up with."

Bruce Murdstone smiled bitterly as he replied, "Our kind, Long? You forget, we left the faith to get away from a forced marriage."

"Forced *bigamous* marriage, you mean, which is now agin the laws of Utah. You kids never broke faith with the Salt Lake Temple. The maniacs who lit out to the desert to defy the real Mormons did. I ain't a Mormon. I like tobacco and other stimulating things too much. But I've worked with some decent Mormon lawmen. I've done a few favors for the Church, and I know some high-placed Elders who owe me. I can send a night letter, explaining your situation and telling them you don't want to live in sin no more. As I see it, the only faith you bent with your Church was living sort of unofficial and dressing your woman in pants. I reckon I can word things so's my pals in Salt Lake could forgive you, provided you got hitched proper in the Temple on arrival."

Billie Murdstone's eyes looked like a kid's outside a candy-store window as she gasped, "Oh, could you do such a thing for us, Mr. Long?"

"I said I would, didn't I? As to the disappointed Elders in your own home town, I've learned that most of the Avenging Angels dumb enough to actually pack a gun are simple souls with a fanatic devotion to what they fancy as the word of Joseph Smith, distorted a mite by twisted Elders. I can see a Mormon Angel gunning for you here in the Dakotas, but an Elder ordering the avenging of two respectable Mormons married in the eyes of the Temple in Salt Lake would have some tall talking to do, and like I said, the Salt Lake law can likely protect you better than the local sheriff would, considering he has you down as a couple of sissy boys."

Bruce hesitated, but Longarm knew Billie would make his mind up for him with some sweet talk on a pillow. So he said, "I'll get back to you after I wire Salt Lake and get it set up for you. Meanwhile, I'll just tear up this particular census report, since it don't make sense and you won't be here much longer. Oh, I forgot to tell you. When I ain't fooling with the census, I'm a U.S. deputy. That's how come I get to send wires for free. It just occurred to me that whilst I'm betraying my trust to the Census Bureau, I might as well put out an all-points bulletin on that Mormon couple that was killed when the Deadwood stage turned over down near Newcastle. I'll have to get Calamity Jane to lie about it too, but don't worry, she enjoys it."

* * *

116

Longarm saw that he wasn't turning out to be an efficient census taker. He tended to get too interested in the conversations. He decided to go on into Lead and backtrack if it turned out that neither of the missing men who'd ridden this trail a while back had gotten that far. He spotted other little spreads on the short ride along the gulch, but there weren't all that many, and if the sheriff's posse had already been over this ground, Longarm knew he could be beating a dead horse. He wasn't going to find any missing men just spoiling in the sun, and he doubted that anyone was likely to just come right out and say that he or she had gunned them. He had to come up with something the local lawmen had missed. He made a mental note to check on how good the so-called sheriff was; he'd have to study on an unincorporated county having a sheriff in the first place. More than one old boy calling himself a sheriff in some out-of-the-way place had turned out to be little more than an outlaw with an inflated ego.

The town law he'd talked to back in Deadwood had been right about the gold camp of Lead not being as big as London or New York. The sprawling mine works of the Homestake claim dominated the slopes with timber chutes, cableways, machine sheds, and such. The cluster of shops and shacks along the bottom of the draw by the railroad yards and the evil-smelling creek were sort of an afterthought. Old Pete Culhane had been right about its being a chore to get ounces of color out of tons of rock, and the hot noon sunlight was hazy with dust too fine to settle and too gritty to breathe. He tethered his chestnut in front of a ramshackle saloon to wet his whistle before he paid any social calls. Had he known things would be so dry and dusty in these parts, he'd have brought water in his canteens instead of Maryland rye. Straight redeye was all right for snakebite and cold night riding, but if a man used it too much for mouthwash, he tended to walk funny.

Longarm never got the beer he had his heart set on, for

a man came out of the saloon, wiping his face with the back of his hand, took one look at Longarm, and lit out like a cat with turpentine under its tail.

Longarm had seen enough of the face to recognize it. It was the station hand who'd mysteriously disappeared after the stage ambush. He was across the tracks and running upslope like an infernal mountain goat. Longarm wanted to talk to him about another slope he'd run up to send smoke signals from, so he lit out after him, and thanks to his long legs and low-heeled army boots, Longarm moved faster than most men his size.

He didn't chase the rascal on his mare, because no horse could scramble over scree and mine tailings like a man afoot. He didn't draw and fire at the jasper because dead men tell no tales, and Longarm wanted to discuss his recent activities with him. So the scared man kept running and Longarm kept chasing, and as they zigzagged up the slope, Longarm saw that he was gaining, although slower than he liked. The mysterious stranger shot a look back over his shoulder, saw the same thing, and cut across the slope toward some mine machinery buildings as he realized that he'd never beat Longarm to the crest.

Naturally, Longarm followed. Something was pounding harder than his own heart in the thin air, and he saw a red sign over the doorway of the towerlike structure the fugitive was making for. It read, "DANGER, KEEP OUT!" but the man ran into the black opening anyway. Longarm didn't know whether he was packing a shooting iron or not, but if he was, he was forted good. So Longarm moved upslope to get out of the field of fire from the opening before he drew his .44 and moved in. He moved cautiously but quickly, knowing the other gent could be out the far side and running like hell if he wasn't up to making a stand. The ground thudded under Longarm's boots and he realized that the structure was a stamping mill, driven by steam and drawing its quartz rock from a long conveyor belt running down the slope a good two stories off the ground.

A window opened in the structure high above Longarm's head, and a man called down, "Hey, what are you doing down there? You want to get kilt?"

Longarm called up, "Not if I can help it. Is there a back way out of that ore crusher?"

"No, and that opening you're facing ain't no damned door, it's a clean-out portal. You're on company property and I'll thank you to haul ass!"

"Not just yet, thanks. I forgot to mention I'm the law. A gent I'm chasing just run into your mill, so if it's all the same to you, I'm going to have a look-see inside. I'd advise you to shut off the machinery; bullets do bounce every which way off revolving gears."

By the time Longarm got to the opening, the stamping mill had stopped hammering itself into the ground. Longarm knew better than to backlight himself in a doorway longer than he had to, so he moved inside fast and slid his back along the rough timber wall to one side as he took in the layout of the place. He found it crowded in there. The whole space was taken up by what looked like the inside of a printing press big enough to use railroad locomotives for type. The jaws were open like the mouth of Jonah's whale, and the mill's mouth was half full of chewed-up rock, sand, and dust. Some rock flour rose like fumes of dry ice from the pile between the big steel jaws, but he could see well enough, now that his eyes were used to the gloom. So he said, "It ain't any use, old son. Wherever you're hiding, you'd best come out. As you see, I'm betwixt you and the only exit. The longer you make me wait, the testier I figure to get."

There was no answer from the surrounding gloom, but a hatch above him opened, and the mining engineer called down, "What's going on down there? I got ore to crush, damn it!"

Longarm looked up the steel ladder to the hatchway and

said, "I can see that. You have a better view than me from up there. Is the rascal over behind that flywheel like I suspicion?"

"Naw, there ain't nobody down there now but you, and this shut-down is starting to vex me."

"Well, hold your vexes while I study this," said Longarm, circling the machinery with a puzzled frown. He had to hug the wall all the way around, and he saw that there was just no place the fugitive could have run, unless—

He placed the toe of his boot gingerly in the crushed ore between the silent, two-story steel jaws. Then he grimaced as he rolled over a rock with blood on it. He called up, "That sign outside was right on the money. He must not have paid much attention to where he was running. He was looking back at me as he ducked in here, as I remember."

"Jesus H. Christ! Are you saying I made sluice out of him?"

"No, he made *himself* fit for further processing. But I doubt he'll pan out with much color, unless he had gold teeth or a valuable watch."

"This is awful. What are we going to do?"

"Don't see as there's much anyone can do now. Any ID on him is paper pulp, and even if we sifted him out of all that sand he's mixed with, I don't reckon his own mother could tell him from strawberry preserves. Why don't you just start up again, and I'll be on my way. Like I said, he might have had at least a gold tooth, so he could pan out higher grade than the rest of the ore in there."

Longarm holstered his gun and walked outside, squinting to get his bearings. As he headed back down the slope, he heard the stamping mill start up again. Waiting at the bottom was a wary-looking gent with a pewter star on the front of his shirt.

Longarm said, "Howdy."

"Howdy your own self," the constable said. "Would you like to tell me how come you're running up and down like that on company property? The Homestake claim is posted, mister."

"I noticed. I ain't a mister. I'm a deputy U.S. marshal. I was chasing a suspect."

"Catch him?"

"No, he caught himself before I could ask polite who hired him. Can we get out of this hot sun? I was fixing to come by your office for a jaw with you in any case."

The local lawman nodded, and as he led the way to the town lockup, Longarm filled him in on the ambushing of the stage and such. The townie led him into a front office and introduced him to his superior, a man named Dalton. The constable he'd met first was called Murphy.

They were good old boys, and treated him decently with some bourbon and branch water. But as they sat around the chief's desk comparing notes, they couldn't offer much help. They knew about the census, of course, but they said nobody had been by to take any in Lead. Longarm described the man he'd chased into the stamping mill, and they said his description didn't ring any bells, but they'd let him know if any of the town regulars turned up missing.

Dalton lit the cigar Longarm had offered in exchange for the drink, and frowned and said, "Your tale's a pure pisser, Longarm. As I see her, you got too many trees for one lone hunter to bark up. You've seen that folks in these parts can act surly to strangers who pester them, so ain't it possible that there's not any deep dark plot, but that the first crew just sort of got lost in a series of misunderstandings?"

Longarm said, "I thought of that. But as I told you, I've been jumped more'n once, just trying to get here. So somebody must not have wanted me to investigate the vanishing census takers. I can see some surly hermit gunning a stranger and tossing him down a mine shaft or planting him in the aspen. But I can't see him staking out every route into the area with a fair-sized gang unless he had something more important to hide than being crazy. I told you, I suspicion that most of the gents I've brushed with were ex-convicts. Does that ring any chimes? I wired both Washington and Pierre about that, and they can't get a handle for me on any sudden rash of early releases from the federal or territorial prison systems."

Dalton shook his head and said, "I know what ex-cons look like. I can't say I've noticed more than the usual here in Lead, and the ones I noticed all went away when the mining company wouldn't hire them. As you can see, this ain't a big town, and mysterious strangers stand out some."

Murphy pursed his lips and said, "I jawed with a mysterious stranger the other night. He didn't look like no ex-convict—more like a man of the cloth, save for the serious-looking brace of Colts he was wearing. He was over to the saloon, asking questions but not drinking. I told him we had a town statute on wearing guns, and he showed me a license issued by Nevada. It was one of them private-detective things like bounty hunters carry. So I told him this wasn't Nevada and that I'd be obliged if he got out of town before I finished my rounds. He must have seen I meant it, for he was gone the next time I looked in."

Longarm raised an eyebrow and asked, "What kind of questions was this gent asking the boys in the saloon, Murph?"

"He was looking for some gal who'd run off from her husband," Murphy replied. "Asked if anyone had noticed a handsome dark blonde gal arriving recent with a dark-headed gent. Said the folks he worked for would pay for such informing."

"What did the locals tell him, Murph?"

"Hell, what was there to tell? There's a lot of blonde gals and dark-headed gents in the territory. But we know 'em all. None of 'em arrived recent."

Longarm finished his drink, rose, and said he had to get back to Deadwood. They didn't try to stop him. He got to his hired mount, forked aboard, and lit out, riding harder than usual until he got back to the Murdstone cabin.

The young Mormon couple came out on the porch as he dismounted in a cloud of dust. Longarm said, "I just cut the trail of an Avenging Angel. They traced you this far, but he must not know you on sight, so Billie had best stay in those britches for now. You two are going to have to light out right now. Do you have a lawyer or somebody you can trust to liquidate this spread for you?"

Bruce nodded and said, "Sure, Lawyer Greenberg in Deadwood is an honest man, for a Gentile. I'll ride in with you and—"

"No you won't. I can remember his name, and you'll have to trust me, too. You two ride for Lead and hop a train. He's already checked out Lead, so he won't be watching for you there. Meanwhile, after I tell your lawyer to sell you out and forward the proceeds in care of the Salt Lake Temple, I'll wire the Mormon Elders I told you about, and they'll be waiting for you at the station with a brass band, or at least a brace of Salt Lake coppers."

He climbed back in the saddle, glared down at them, and asked, "What in thunder are you waiting for? Pack your possibles and clear out! I can't be everywhere at once. If I miss the Angel in my travels, he could run into somebody who gossips, or just stumble over you while backtracking."

Billie gasped, "Oh, how will we ever be able to thank you?"

But her man frowned and said, "I'm not afraid of one man."

Longarm grimaced and said, "You're dumber than you look, then. No offense, but you're a cowhand, not a gunslick, and the gent that's after you is a fanatic who's been chose to kill folks for the Lord. You may not be scared of him, but I sure am. I've run into his kind before."

"Can you arrest him, Deputy Long?"

"I don't know. He might be too good for me. It's unconstitutional to bounty-hunt folks that ain't wanted anywhere by the law. If that won't stick, I'll think of something else. Meanwhile, you two get your innocent selves back to Salt Lake, where you'll be safe. It's been nice meeting you, but I got chores, and if I ever see either of you in this territory again, I'll have to arrest you for your own protection."

Chapter 10

By the time Longarm had seen the Murdstones' lawyer and sent his wires to Salt Lake and other places, it was getting close to suppertime. It was a caution how the day had flown, considering the little he'd gotten done. He'd told Redfern he'd meet up with the rest of the census crew at suppertime, so he headed back to the hotel. As he was crossing the street, a voice yelled out, "Longarm, you old bastard! Tarnation, if you ain't a sight for sore eyes!"

He turned and said, "Howdy, Calamity. I had a good lie for you to tell about the stage getting turned over, but all's well that ends well, and you can just tell folks the truth now, if you got it in you."

"I tolt the reporters I shot *all* the rascals. I hope you don't mind, honey bun? I meant to tell things as they happened, but as I was jawing about it, my words just took the bit in their teeth and run away with a few details."

He knew nobody believed her, no matter what she said, and he didn't worry about his rep, so he just grinned and said, "Well, hell, as I remember, you was shooting every which ways, so you could have dropped the two of 'em."

"Uh, Longarm, it was a *dozen* of 'em I got, now that I study on what I told them reporters. I mean, who's to say, since the owlhoots come back and stole all the bodies, right?"

"A dozen makes a nice round number, Calamity. But I got to be on my way now."

"Where you going, honey bun? Would you fancy coming home with me for some home cooking, white lightning, and other entertainments?"

"Not right now thanks. I'm meeting some folks, official, over to the Palace."

"Can I sort of tag along, honey bun?"

"Not hardly, no offense. It's a private meeting."

"Would you be willing to be seed in public with me if I went home and put on a she-male dress?"

He was too polite to answer truthfully, so he repeated that it was official and that he was on a secret mission. He left her standing there like a lost pup. He tried not to feel sorry for her, since she'd chosen of her own free will to drink herself into the state she was in. But she wasn't a bad old gal, even if she was loco, and it seemed a shame what liquor, clap, and the cruel shark of Time could do to a once-innocent country gal.

He was late getting to supper, so Redfern and the others had started without him. Longarm sat down and felt better about being late when he tasted what the Palace called supper. Redfern introduced him all around. The census crew were the green-looking hands he figured they'd be. Naturally, they were all male, though a couple of them looked unsure whether to stand or squat when they took a leak. But they were all bright-eyed and bushy-tailed to ride out and pester folks with their fool questionnaires. Longarm said it was fixing to get dark in the first place, and that he meant to get them some local help in the second. "My trial run showed me that taking a census in these parts could be dangerous for a man's health, even if somebody wasn't plotting against the census," he told them.

He looked about for Redfern's wife and stepson, but didn't ask, of course, why they weren't invited to eat with the menfolk. Redfern sniffed and said, "I don't know what explanation I'm going to give for these delays, Long."

"Blame 'em on me," Longarm said. "It was Washington's notion to have me riding herd on you, and like I said, I ain't letting any of you pilgrims out to get bushwacked till I have a better handle on the whos and whys."

He reached for a roll, but gave up on the notion when he hefted it; it was as heavy as adobe and just as dry. "I was just over to the telegraph office," he said. "Picked up an answer to a question I sent out last night. You're right that this year's census is almost finished everywhere else. But look on the bright side. They've been having trouble out in California too. They got other deputies investigating that messed-up census, since I can only spread myself so thin. But it's sort of spooky to study on."

Redfern frowned and said, "I hadn't heard. Are you saying someone's been resisting the census in California too?"

"I did. I must not have spoke clear enough with these infernal spuds in my mouth. Some old boys rode out to ask questions in the Mother Lode country, with the same results. Only this time they found one of them, up near Angel's Camp. He was down an abandoned mineshaft. He didn't fall in. Somebody'd shot him first. In the back."

One of the Easterners threw his napkin on the table and got up. "That tears it! I don't know about the rest of you, but I'm going back East tonight! They don't pay enough on this job for a man to get shot!"

There was a mutter of agreement, and Redfern looked

stricken. He turned to Longarm and said, "Now look what you've done, damn it!"

"I didn't do it. Somebody else is gunning census takers here and other places. I know I'm supposed to be a heroic gent, so I ain't fixing to cut out on you. But fair is fair, and I'm paid to take such chances. I can't say I'd shame a man who dropped out of the game because he never signed on to get shot at."

One of the others said, "Oh, hell, I'll stay for now," and a couple of others agreed with him. It just went to show that you couldn't read a book by its cover. The one who volunteered to see it through was a little runt wearing glasses. The one who was making squaw-talk about cutting out was almost as big as Longarm and had a tough-looking face.

They batted the California story back and forth as they finished supper. Then, having done his duty with them for now, Longarm left to go get something to eat. As he was leaving, the dark, sardonic Redfern followed him out to the veranda and said, "I didn't want to say so inside, my crew is already edgy enough, but don't the Hearsts have holdings in the Mother Lode country of California?"

"I'm ahead of you on that angle. So's Washington. Senator George Hearst ain't in California or Nevada. He's in Washington, on some sort of committee holding special sessions about one thing and another."

"For God's sake, no U.S. senator's about to do his own dirty work! And you told me you suspect that the men you gunned had been released from prison recently by someone with political pull."

"I know what I told you, Redfern. I was listening too, at the time. It do seem interesting that somebody don't want Uncle Sam to know who's living near at least two of Senator Hearst's mining operations. But the old senator's been around a long time, and nobody's ever caught him killing anybody yet. They're an old California family, respected by folks who don't even like 'em. I can't see them turning into mad-dog killers at this late date, can you?"

"Then maybe he's a victim, like us?"

"That makes more sense. I know the country around their California holdings; I chased some highgraders over it some a while back. It's sort of like the country around here. Rough and sparse-populated. But as far as anyone can tell, neither the Sheep Ranch mine nor the Homestake has been having union troubles, none of their miners are missing, they ain't being highgraded, and Lord knows you don't jump the claim of a U.S. senator as powerful as old George Hearst. I hear he's sort of upset about it, though. Soon as he can wind up his chores with the special summer session, he's headed out this way with a posse of Pinkertons to find out what in hell's going on about his holdings.

"I want to catch the sheriff before he gets drunk. See you later."

"I'd like to go with you, if you don't mind," Redfern said.

"I fear I do mind. Why don't you stay here and keep your wife and kid company?"

Redfern laughed bitterly and said, "David Boggs is not my son, thank God, and as for Penny, she's got the sulks again. Say, is it true what they say about the ladies of the evening in this town?"

"The only whore I know well enough to introduce you to is Calamity Jane, and you don't look that desperate. You'll have to make your own arrangements, friend. I'm a U.S. deputy, not a pimp."

Redfern's face darkened and he gasped, "See here, just who do you think you're talking to, Long?"

Longarm said, "You ought to know who you are better than me. I don't look at your face in the mirror when I shave of a morning."

Then he walked away before Redfern could get the notion he didn't like him much.

An hour later, Longarm decided he didn't like Sheriff Mahoney worth mention, either. He'd caught up with Mahoney in the Buckhorn Saloon, and the big red-faced gent looked sober enough, considering the hour. But when Longarm told him what he wanted, Mahoney scowled at him. "I ain't got the hands to spare. Even if I had, why should I have a deputy riding with each and every damned old census taker?"

"To keep 'em from getting murdered, of course. Don't you want your poor old Uncle Sam to know how many folks hang out in these parts, Sheriff?"

"Why should I, as long as they behave themselves? I looked for them jaspers as turned up missing, dammit. Looking for lost children goes with the job. But playing nursemaid don't. Them census dudes is federal employees. Why can't you gents from the marshal's office ride herd on 'em?"

"Some other federal deputies are due any minute, but meanwhile they ain't here, and I can only watch one back at a time. By the way, I've been meaning to ask you how a gent gets elected sheriff in an unincorporated county."

Mahoney laughed easily and said, "I admire a man who threatens delicate, Longarm. But it won't wash. You can wire Pierre if you like, and they'll tell you the territorial government approved my provisional status. We're set up provisional here. That means—"

"I know what a provisional government is," Longarm cut in. "Of course, if any irregularities showed up in the voting records and such between now and the time you get full status, the territory might provide you boys with another government entire, right?"

Mahoney's smile faded as he said, "You can go to hell and take your kin with you! Don't try and twist my arm with bullshit about proper elections. The election board in

Pierre investigated ahead of you, and while a few names was throwed out for bad spelling or being off a tombstone, most of the offenses was committed by the other party, so Pierre says we won fair enough for these parts."

Longarm sighed and said, "I know. I checked it out." Then he spotted someone in the mirror over the bar and said, "I reckon I can't make you help out with the census, seeing as you're so busy with that bourbon. But I'm fixing to mayhaps make an arrest. You want in on it?"

"Depends on who you're talking about. I generally let the town law pick folks up here in Deadwood. But the whole county's under my jurisdiction if it's somebody important."

Longarm nodded and said, "Don't turn around, but take a gander in yon mirror at the gent in the corner wearing a dusty black suit and a brace of Colts. See him?"

"Yeah, looks like a preacher or a whiskey drummer, save for the hardware. Is there a reward on him?"

"Don't reckon. Why?"

"He's all yours, Longarm. I don't want him for nothing, and he looks mean enough to curdle milk."

Longarm thanked the sheriff for his cooperation and walked over to the man seated at a table in the corner. There were neither drinks nor cards on the table, so Longarm put his glass on it and sat down, saying, "Howdy."

The man in the rusty black suit moved into the corner, hiding his guns from view as he stared soberly at Longarm and said, "I don't drink, sir."

"That's all right. I ain't inviting. My handle is Custis Long and I'm a U.S. deputy."

"Oh, yes, I've heard of you. You're the one they call Longarm. I understand you've killed a lot of men in the name of the law."

"That could be true. How many have you killed in the name of whatever, and do you have a name or am I supposed to guess?"

"You can call me Brother William, if you must. I assume

131

you want to see my license from the state of Nevada?"

"No, thanks, I've seen bounty-hunting papers before. I'll 'fess right out I know who you are from the law in Lead. It saves time to spread the cards out on the table right off, even if you don't play cards."

Brother William stared dead-eyed at Longarm for a time before he said, "I am a member of the Latter-Day Saints, if that's what you're twitting me about."

"I ain't twitting you, Brother William. I'm trying to figure out what you're doing in Deadwood. There ain't a Mormon Temple here."

"If you must know, I have a warrant for the recapture of a runaway bride and the arrest of her abductor. Do you want to see it?"

"Not hardly. It can't be any good in Dakota, no matter how it reads. I didn't know elopement was on the Nevada books as a criminal offense."

"I follow a higher law than the state of Nevada," said Brother William, smug enough to make a cat puke.

Longarm nodded and said, "I figured you might be an Angel. I know this is likely a waste of time, but I read a lot. So one weekend in Salt Lake when I had nothing else on hand, I tried my luck with *The Book of Mormon*."

"I'll not have you sneer at the revelations of the Prophet, Joseph Smith!"

"Simmer down. I wouldn't sneer at a Chinaman's Good Book, if I could read it. I'd be a liar if I said I went along with everything Joseph Smith had to say. That's likely 'cause I was raised to another Good Book, the one King James had something to do with. But I read *The Book of Mormon* respectful, and some of it made a heap of sense. Anyone can see the Smith brothers was decent men at heart."

Brother William smiled like a recently hanged man and said, "That's a very generous attitude, coming from a Gentile."

"Well, fair is fair, and like I said, you folks don't have

a faith any ornerier than most. I disremember your Prophet putting anything down on paper about holding women in bondage or gunning young gents for falling in love. I got the impression Joseph Smith was a gentle-hearted soul who approved of Faith, Hope, Charity, and all the other stuff most religious folks go in for."

Brother William shrugged and said, "The Prophet Joseph and his brother were lynched by persecuting Gentiles before the rest of us fled West. In the face of persecution, our Church has had to amend some of his teachings in a more Old Testament fashion."

Longarm shook his head and said, "The main Temple in Salt Lake's amended things back to abiding by the law of the land. I wasn't out here during the Mormon Wars, and it's not for me to say who was right or wrong at Mountain Meadows. But Utah and the rest of the country have been getting along much better lately."

The Avenging Angel said, "You're right, it's not for you to say. Is there any point to this tedious religious argument, Longarm?"

"We ain't having a religious argument. I'm telling you as a federal lawman that your unholy writ don't run in Dakota. So if you shoot anybody close enough to startle me, I'll arrest you or worse before the smoke clears. Do you follow my drift, or do I have to say it clearer?"

Brother William shook his head and smiled, but his eyes glittered like a weasel's in a henhouse as he said, "Oh, I understand you perfectly. The Murdstones are in these parts, and they've approached the federal law for help. I thank you, Longarm. I'd about given up on the trail that led me here to Deadwood."

Longarm opened his mouth to say something. Then he shut it when he realized how dumb he was. Billie and Bruce would have left by now, so the Avenging Angel had nobody in Deadwood to avenge, and the longer he stayed here the better. So Longarm nodded and said, "When you're right you're right, Brother William. The kids you've been haunting are under my personal protection as well as Uncle Sam's. So if you run into them, you'd best leave them alone, savvy?"

"I will do what my Lord commands."

Longarm finished his drink, blew some smoke in the killer's face, and got up to go find someone sensible to talk to. He spotted one of the Deadwood Dicks coming in with Calamity Jane, and they talked even crazier than the Avenging Angel, so he looked about for an escape route. Then he stopped and thought for a moment, and went back to the bar to order another drink.

Sure enough, Calamity spotted him and came over. He was glad she hadn't brought Deadwood Dick. Calamity was enough of a chore to talk to, and he already knew that both Deadwood Dicks could miss a man-sized target from three feet away.

Calamity Jane said, "Here you are, you rascal. You promised me a drink, remember?"

He nodded and signaled the barkeep, who looked surprised but served her anyway. He let her inhale some redeye before he said, "I got a favor to ask you, Calamity."

"Hot gullywashers! What do you want from me, lover cuss?"

"I'm in the market for some professional help, Calamity."

"Nobody screws more professional than me, you sweet, hot, and horny thing. I used to do it for a living."

"Damn it, Calamity, dogs and dragonflies know how to screw. Screwing is easier than what I have in mind."

She looked wistfully down at her empty glass as she sighed and answered, "Easy for you, mayhaps. I don't seem to be so popular with the boys of late. But tell me about this more complicated notion of your'n, and if it don't sound too painful, I reckon I'm game."

He signaled the barkeep with two fingers as he said,

"Despite your way with words, you do know how to handle that hogleg you pack under that coat, and just as important, you can't be that unpopular hereabouts, or you wouldn't still be alive. I want to deputize you and some Deadwood old-timers who know the country and the folks around it well enough to keep from getting swatted like flies. Don't mention either of the Deadwood Dicks. I already know neither of them can hit a man-sized target from three feet away. If anybody you drink with has wanted flyers out on them, I don't need to hear about it. Do you figure you can rustle me up such a band on short notice, Calamity?"

She picked up her refilled shotglass and said, "Who are we riding agin, Longarm? I tolt you about the time I saved Buffalo Bill from the Sioux, didn't I?"

"I don't want to hear it again any more than Bill Cody does. We ain't riding agin anybody, and hopefully they won't come at us. But if they do, I want at least two mean-looking locals riding with each and every census taker when I turn them loose to count noses, come sunrise. Any damn fool can bushwhack a greenhorn riding alone in strange country, but with a little help from your friends, I mean to make the rascals work at gunning any more. In case all eight of the crew are still here in the morning, I'll need at least sixteen hard and dangerous-looking characters, counting yourself, no offense."

Calamity said, "Buy me another whilst I study on it. There's Blackie Slade and Walleyed McQueen, just lost their jobs when the mine bottomed out. If you're paying for these services, I could ask old No-Nose Nolan if he was in or not. You must remember Noseless from your salad days in Dodge, right?"

"I do, and I'll pay a dollar a day if they bring their own bullets. But No-Nose is getting on in years, ain't he, Calamity?"

"Hell, sweet youth, all of us gets on in years if somebody don't kill us first, and a lot of men have made the serious mistake of trying to kill old No-Nose. He may be getting on in years, but he's as ugly as his face, in any kind of fight."

Longarm signaled the barkeep again and said they might as well all save useless motions by leaving the bottle handy. He told Calamity Jane, "All right, I know No-Nose Nolan scares me, so he'll likely do. Are you sure all these gents will throw in with you, Calamity? I don't want to be rude, but you may have noticed some folks fail to take you as serious as they likely should, since you've become a regular feature in Ned Buntline's penny-dreadfuls."

Calamity Jane refilled her glass as she sighed, "I know. But when I tell 'em you're in command and paying a dollar a day, they'll jump at the chance. It's been getting mighty tedious in Deadwood since we hanged the last claim jumper and they built that infernal church down the draw."

He left her to finish the bottle and figure out where to round up the men he needed, saying he'd check back with her later.

It was fairly dark out now, so the town was starting to come alive. Longarm stepped back politely as a couple of men loped through town firing their sixguns at the moon. They looked like cowboys. Deadwood was getting civilized enough to have cowboys, now that they'd started raising stock on the range all about. He knew they wouldn't get in any trouble unless they took to aiming at street-lamps and windows instead of the moon. So after they'd passed, he went on his way, headed back to his hotel. He needed a bath and a change of underwear.

He wondered if the Dill sisters had left a lamp burning in their cabin window for him, and then wondered why he was wondering about that. If he'd left any part of either one of them unexplored, he couldn't think what he'd missed, and he had no call to feel horny again so soon.

Nobody Longarm knew was in the lobby, so he fished out his key as he went up the stairs and down the second-story hallway to his hired room. He spied a length of match-stick on the hall runner near his door. It didn't belong there. He'd wedged the matchstick in the doorjamb near the hinges on going out, just so he'd know, like right now, if anyone had opened the door while he was out.

He drew his .44 and quietly tried the knob. The door was unlocked. He twisted it, kicked the door open, and moved in fast and low, crabbing to one side as he said, "Freeze, whoever you may be!"

Then, by the wan light of the candlestick on the bedtable, he saw Redfern's wife, Penny, leap up from the bed like it was a hot stove. Her long blonde hair was unbound and hanging down the front of her kimono. She gasped, "Oh, you startled me!"

He holstered the .44 as he shut the door behind him and said, "You startled me too. Just like your husband might, if he comes by to find you and me in this situation, Miss Penny. By the way, just what *is* this situation, and where's little David?"

"David's asleep down the hall, bless his heart. As to Howard coming back to say one thing or another, he won't. I don't know which parlor house he went to tonight, but he generally spends the whole night there."

Longarm took off his Stetson but kept his other duds on and stayed at a safe distance as he said, "What your man does on his own time is betwixt you and him, Miss Penny."

She said, "I know. You *were* the man on the train with that awful woman in the egret hat, weren't you?"

"Don't speak ill of the dead. She wasn't that awful. What's my personal life got to do with yours, Miss Penny?"

"I want you to make love to me. I want to pay Howard back by throwing myself at the lowest man I know in town."

"Thanks. I happen to be taller than your rambling How-ard. I ain't sure who's acting lowest here. I disremember asking a married woman to bust any commandments, sis. Seems to me it was your notion, not mine."

She moved closer, allowing the kimono to fall open, which, even in such dim light, had a more inspiring effect than he'd expected. She was built better than she let on when fully clad. He noticed she was blonde all over, but he still insisted, "Hold on now. I've met up with gals who played your wicked game before, and I reckon I'd just as soon sit this one out. Can't you find somebody else to get revenge with?"

She said, "Not as good looking, and not with your, ah, references. I couldn't help hearing, on that train, and I must say you and that hussy had amazing stamina."

"I was questioning a suspect in the line of duty. This here would be plain old-fashioned adultery."

"Oh? Is that against the Code of the West?"

"It's against mine. You can call me a sissy, but a man has to draw the line somewhere and mine's drawn at married women, if I know their husbands."

"Howard will never know."

"Maybe not. But you will. I will. I can see it bothers you less than it does me. If you're so mad at old Howard, why don't you leave him like a sport instead of playing jolly tit-for-tat when anyone can see you're heart ain't in it?"

She looked surprised and sort of hurt as she asked, "Is it that obvious? I had a couple of good stiff drinks before I came down the hall to tempt you."

"I noticed. It ain't the liquor on your breath. It's the scared look in your eyes. By the way, how in thunder did you unlock my door?"

"I wiggled my own key in the lock, and as I suspected, these locks are pretty cheap. I guess I half hoped I wouldn't be able to get in. But I had to at least make the effort. How did you know this was the first time I'd done this sort of thing?"

"Male intuition. Your man said you hadn't been married long. You still ain't said why the hell you don't just leave him if he's all that much a bother."

She sat on the bed, defeated, and hung her head as she told the rug, "I've a child to feed and no place to go. He's stingy as well as a brute. I have exactly thirty-seven cents left over from our train trip here. How far do you think David and I could get on thirty-seven cents?"

"Depends on where you had to go to. Do you have anyone, anywhere, who'd take you and the boy in, Miss Penny?"

"Of course. My parents in Ohio. But Ohio may as well be the moon. And Howard would just follow, like he did the last time I tried to leave him. He beat me that time, in front of David. I couldn't go through that again."

Longarm shrugged and said, "You sure have a hard old row to hoe, honey. I've hit lucky in a couple of gunfights lately, but there'd be no sense buying you a ticket if you ain't up to getting aboard."

She looked up defiantly and said, "Damn it, I think I'll take you up on that! If I could get all the way back to my dad and brothers in Ohio, my child and I would be out of his reach forever. Could you advance me enough for fare and a half and maybe something to eat on the way?"

He shrugged and said, "Advance it, hell. When you never expect to see money again, you ain't advancing, you're giving. But what the hell, I don't like him, either, and if I find out at breakfast that this was just a sob story, please don't laugh at me in front of the others."

She nodded soberly and said, "All right, we have a deal."

Then she slipped out of the kimono and met his gaze with her own.

Longarm shook his head and said, "I suspicion you didn't understand my offer, Miss Penny. I ain't out to buy your body. I want to buy the freedom of an abused wife and child."

"Don't you want me?"

"Hell, of course I want you. I'm a human being and you

must have seen yourself at least once in the mirror. But let's count out the cash and say no more about it. There's a midnight train headed south to the transcontinental connection, so you and the boy have a good four or five hours to get ready. I'd let the kid sleep a mite first. I ain't named Vanderbilt, so coach seats is all I can afford when I'm paying out of my own pocket."

He took out his wallet and removed the wherewithal to see her and the kid to maybe Penn State if Ohio wasn't still there. He handed it to her, feeling awkward about even innocently handing money to a naked lady.

She stared down in wonder at the wad of bills in her small fist, and gasped, "That much? And with no strings attached? I can't believe it! Up to now, I've never gotten anything this generous from a man who wasn't after my . . . you know."

"Maybe you've been hanging around with the wrong kind of men, then. And I admire your you-know a heap, now that I've seen it. But you can put your duds back on now."

She slipped the kimono back on, sort of, as she shook her head and asked in a bewildered tone, "Why are you doing this for me, Custis? I'm nothing to you."

He said, "You're wrong. You ain't a nothing. You're a human being in trouble. I'm in a position to help. I don't see it as all that hard to savvy."

She rose, letting the kimono fall to the floor around her feet as she came to him, took him in her arms, and sighed, "I was wrong about you. You're not the rough-and-ready yokel I first took you for. You're a real gentleman."

He would have said, "Aw, mush." But she was kissing him, so he couldn't.

He ran his hands up her naked spine as she plastered her nude breasts against the rough wool of his vest. But then, before he could figure his next move, the sound of gunfire came in through the window. He let go of her, snuffed the

140

candle, and opened the blinds as she gasped, "What happened? Can you see, Mr. Long?"

"I can see out. But I can't see what happened. Might be those drunk cowboys riding through again. Might be something more important. I'd best go down and make sure. It's been nice meeting up with you, Penny."

As he moved for the door, snagging his hat, Penny asked, "What about us?" and he said, "Us wasn't meant to happen, for I told you I don't trifle with married women, no matter what I think of their husbands. Your train leaves at midnight, Penny. You and young David had best be on it."

It wasn't hard to tell where the shots had come from. Everyone on the street was headed that way. He fell in beside a townie to ask, "What happened, pard?"

"Ain't sure, but there seems to have been a shootout down near Madam Goldie's place."

Longarm slowed dow. A personal dispute over a woman of the town could get serious, but it wasn't a federal offense to shoot folks in or about cathouses. He knew if he had a lick of sense he'd stay clear of it. But he had normal curiosity, so he drifted with the crowd.

He saw Sheriff Mahoney and a couple of town lawmen standing over a body lying facedown in the dusty street. The light from a nearby window revealed the checkered suit of the dead man. A big gray cat got up and stretched in Longarm's gut as he moved closer. Sure enough, as they rolled the obviously dead man over, he saw it was Howard Redfern.

Longarm hung back as he heard one of the lawmen asking if anyone had seen the shootout. A townie volunteered, "It warn't no shootout, Sheriff. The gent was walking across to Madam Goldie's, innocent, when somebody blasted him from over there in the shadows of that livery. Sounded like a pistol, but it could have been a carbine."

Mahoney said, "Check over there, Flynn." And as the

other lawman left to search the shadows for whatever could be there at this late date, the sheriff spotted Longarm in the crowd and said, "Stay out of this, Uncle Sam. I don't need your nose in my beeswax, if it's all the same to you."

Longarm turned away with a nod as he heard Mahoney saying, "We'll take him to the coroner and lay him on ice till someone comes forward to identify him. This shooting folks on weeknights has to stop, dammit!"

Longarm headed back to the hotel, wondering whether Mahoney was too dumb to look for ID in a dead man's pockets or just wanted the wallet and its contents for himself when he could peruse them at leisure.

He didn't know how Penny was going to take this latest development in her already unhappy marriage. He decided it was just as well not to pester her with it. Come morning, she and her kid would be long gone and she wouldn't have to weep false tears in front of the coroner. He knew that if she showed her true feelings they'd likely suspect her. He'd have done so, but she had an alibi.

That left a whole townful of other folks who could have done it. Howard Redfern hadn't been a likable cuss, but he hadn't been in Deadwood long enough to make serious enemies unless, as that townie had suggested, it had been over a woman. As he put it together, old Howard had been touring the barrooms, looking for a good time, and someone had shot him in the back before he found it. Whorehouse fights seldom happened in the middle of the main street, and when they did, the arguers were generally facing one another. It looked more like the crew chief of the Deadwood census had been bushwhacked by someone too anxious to wait for him outside of town. Whoever it was had sure played Ned with the census.

Meanwhile, he still intended to freshen up before he went out again to find out how many old gunhands Calamity Jane could manage. He'd figure out at breakfast if they still needed them.

He saw by the slit of light under his door that Penny had lit the candle before leaving. That had been a fool trick, in a wood-built hotel. He hadn't had time to play match tricks. So he just opened the door and let himself in. Penny hadn't gone off leaving the candlestick lit. She was still there, in bed, under the covers. Her kimono was draped over a chair.

Longarm locked the door behind him, braced the other chair under the knob, and commenced to solemnly remove his gun rig and everything else. "What was going on outside?" Penny asked.

He said, "Whatever it was, it's over and done with."

"Oh, are you taking off your clothes to make love to me?"

"I wasn't figuring on beating you up. You had your chance to leave pure, Penny. I told you I was human."

"Oh, you have a lovely body, too. What made you change your mind? I thought you didn't make love to married women?"

He snuffed out the candle before he lifted the covers to get beside her on the mattress, saying, "I don't, ah, generally."

And then he took her in his arms, and as she felt what he'd been saving up for her pressed between her thighs, she opened them with a happy cry and crooned, "Oh, Lord, now I know what that brunette on the train was making such a fuss over!"

As she responded to his first thrusts with her love-starved pelvis, he knew she'd be easier than most to pleasure. From the way she was pulsating around his shaft, he sensed that her late and damfool husband had been neglecting his chores around the house recently.

He'd told her the truth about avoiding married women as much as he could. But he'd had considerable experience with widows. Having been married twice and knowing her way up and down a man's tool, she moved well. But she wasn't the kind of woman who liked acrobatic fornication.

143

She needed it persistent but tender, with lots of reassuring kisses and no dirty talk in her well-brought-up little ears. So that was the way he treated her, no doubt saving himself a wrenched back; old-fashioned or not, she was built stronger than she appeared, and she punched pretty hard with her pubis.

She gasped, "Oh, Lord, I can't hold out another second!"

"Let her rip, then, honey. I don't mind," he said, and moved a little faster as he felt her climaxing on his erection. She stiffened her spine, bit her lip, and moaned in orgasm before she suddenly went limp and sobbed, "Oh, that was lovely. I wish it wasn't over."

He kissed her throat and growled, "Now who said anything about it being over?" He hooked his toes under the footrail of the bed for purchase and started pounding harder, now that he had her warmed up right.

Penny's eyes opened wide in wonder. "My God, is it possible to do it twice in a row?" She gasped, and then, wrapping her legs around his waist, tried to crush his spine with her soft calves, and added, "Oh, lovely! I see it is!"

He kept his thoughts about her previous lovers to himself.

Penny sobbed, moaned, and rolled her head from side to side, thrashing the pillows with her dark blonde hair as she begged him not to stop and marveled at her multiple climaxes, which she didn't have to tell him about, but did anyway. He finally got there himself, and it was so good it almost hurt.

As he lay throbbing atop her, she murmured, "Oh, I felt that. Have I pleased you, darling?"

"Not yet," he said, for, to his pleased surprise, he was still as stiff as a poker. He had no idea what in thunder Howard Redfern had expected to find in that whorehouse, considering what he'd been neglecting here.

Naturally, it took him even longer the second time, and he'd lost count of how many times she'd climaxed by the time he enjoyed a long, shuddering orgasm in her sweet flesh. When he moved in her experimentally, he noted to his chagrin that his infernal tool was starting to let him down. But she misread his motion and pleaded, "Not again! I don't think I can take any more!"

So he kissed her and said, "Well, all right, I'll have mercy on you."

She didn't get it. She thanked him for being so understanding as he rolled off to enjoy a smoke, with her head pillowed on his shoulder and her hair spread over his damp and heaving chest.

After a long sweet while, she asked him what time it was. He told her and she sighed, "I wish my train wasn't leaving at midnight. Isn't there a later one?"

"Not till nine in the morning, Penny. Leaving then could get complicated."

She shuddered against him and said, "I know. I want to be well on my way with David before Howard even guesses we've left. What if he comes after us again?"

"He won't. I aim to keep him here for a spell."

He started to ask for her home address, so he could write to her later and tell her that she and the boy had nothing to worry about, and that she could forget filing for an expensive divorce. But if he had her address, she'd expect him to write regularly. Anyway, she'd read about her husband's death in the papers when he got around to announcing it.

So he held her close and finished his smoke, and they spent their last few moments together in warm silence.

Chapter 11

Calamity Jane Canary was sitting at a table against the back wall of the saloon with Blackie Slade, Walleyed McQueen, No-Nose Nolan, and a couple of other gents as Longarm came through the swinging doors at half past midnight. Longarm recognized Lonesome Jones from Dodge, and preferred *not* to recognize old Widowmaking Wilson, since, although that Wells Fargo job hadn't been a federal offense, a peace officer wasn't supposed to associate with known criminals. Calamity spotted him in the doorway and called out to him, and then, as he moved across the sawdust-covered floor, she yelled, "Longarm! Duck!"

He dove headfirst to the sawdust and rolled under a table as, above him, enough bullets for a Mexican rebellion whipped through the air!

As the fusillade subsided, Longarm peered out into the reeking gunsmoke, gun in hand, and since the saloon was so filled with blue haze that he couldn't see his hand before his face, he got to his feet and called out, "Hey, Calamity? If you're still alive, I sure wish you'd tell me what's going on!"

She called back, "It ain't no more. Some rascal started to draw on you from behind. But I figure one of us must have hit him, for he don't seem to be firing now worth mention."

As the smoke thinned, Longarm saw Calamity Jane and her five male companions on their feet, guns trained on an overturned, bullet-riddled table in the far corner. The wall above the table was pocked as though a *rurale* firing squad had just been at work. He could tell by the red smear running down the wall that someone had been against it when all six of them fired. He whistled softly and strode over to have a peek over the tabletop.

Brother William lay there, looking surprised about being full of bullet holes as well as dead. The whole front of his black suit was spoiled by what looked like spilled beet preserves, but since the dead man held a Colt.45 in either lifeless fist, Longarm didn't feel as sorry for him as he might have.

Calamity Jane came over, trailed by the others as they reloaded, and said, "Are you all right, honey bun? I thought you was going out like poor old Jim when the rascal followed you in, slapping leather as he crabbed along the wall. Who in tarnation was he, and how come you're so popular?"

Longarm said, "He was a fanatic I had a religious talk with earlier with this evening. I didn't know he'd took our discussion so serious."

Widowmaking Wilson holstered his S&W double-action .38 and said, "Old Calamity here says you're paying a dollar a day for gunhands. You want me to show you how good I can shoot?"

Longarm said, "You just did. She told you true, Widowmaking. But, no offense, I'd best put you on the payroll under another name."

Wilson grinned and said, "Aw, Longarm, I was nowhere near that durned old Wells Fargo office when it got robbed."

"Hush your face," Longarm said, "and don't mention Wells Fargo around me again, savvy?"

Before Widowmaking Wilson could reply, the town lawman whom Longarm had talked to earlier came in, looked down at the corpse, and said, "Jesus H. Christ! What did he run into, stampeding woodpeckers? He's punctured awful, considering it's a weeknight."

Longarm explained the misunderstanding and promised that nobody there would shoot Brother William anymore. So the town law said, "Well, seeing as you are the law and he'd been asked by more than one lawman to vacate the Dakotas, I reckon the coroner will list it as misadventure. But we sure have had us a busy night."

Longarm nodded and said, "Speaking of coroners, I've been meaning to have a word with your friendly Sheriff Mahoney about the dead man in the checkered suit."

The town law said, "Forget it. Mahoney says the case is closed."

"Oh? He identified the body on his own? Funny, I didn't think he looked that smart."

"I'm only guessing, but it looks like there must have been papers out on the rascal in the checked suit. Mahoney denies it and says we know he'd split with us townies. But you know the old saw about rank having its privileges."

"Yeah, he does act sort of self-confident. Where can I find him and the fellow in the checkered suit at the moment, the coroner's?"

"Nope. Sheriff's gone home. Body's gone too."

"What do you mean, the body's gone? Mahoney didn't carry it home with him, did he?"

"Nope. Put it on the midnight train for somewhere. In a box, of course."

Longarm grimaced as he thought of Penny and little David riding behind the baggage car, not knowing the man they were fleeing was on the train with them, getting stiffer by the mile. He said, "That don't make sense. Mahoney run off before I could get around to mentioning it, but I was acquainted with the dead man. He was the head of the government census crew."

"Do tell? You'd best ask Mahoney why he shipped him off, then. He never told us. You know how testy he gets when you ask him questions."

A man in a red flannel shirt and a black beard came in, saw Calamity Jane, and said, "Howdy, Calamity. Heard you was looking for me. I don't want to kiss you, but a dollar a day sounds reasonable."

Calamity Jane said, "Longarm, meet up with Hellfire Hank. Hellfire used to skin for Buffalo Bill, and he's even meaner than he looks."

So Longarm put the mysterious business about missing corpses on the back burner for the moment and explained things to his latest recruit. The town law said he'd get somebody from the coroner's office to neaten up the corner, so they all went to the back and sat around a bottle of Maryland rye that the taxpayers were going to pay for.

As Longarm explained his plans, others summoned by Calamity Jane drifted in. Longarm was glad Marshal Vail would only get to see the names and not the faces of the cutthroat crew he was recruiting to help the census out. There was more than one old boy in the crowd whom Longarm knew he really ought to arrest. But they hadn't sent him all this way to pick up unimportant cow thieves, road agents, casual stabbers, and such. It was surprising how many hardcased-looking folks there were in such a small, out-of-the-way community. None of them remembered any sidekicks who'd been released recently from prison, so, if they were telling the truth, he could likely count on them to back his play. And if the other side had a lick of sense, they wouldn't try to vanish any census takers around *this* ornery bunch!

Next morning, it didn't look like there was going to be any census after all. The greenhorns from back East were spooked by the piratical-looking crew Longarm had lined up in front of the hotel, and by the way Howard Redfern, their boss, had apparently lit out.

"Hell," Longarm said, "he didn't desert the ship, boys. He was only murdered. Didn't any of you hear him getting shot last night?"

One of them, said, "Hell, they fire off their guns at flies out here. What do you mean, Redfern was murdered?"

"The rascal's deader than a turd in a milk bucket. He was gunned down over by Madam Goldie's, but seeing as he's a married man, we'd best drop it there for now. They're still working on who killed him and why. But getting back to taking the census—"

Another shouted, "Bullshit! *You* take the census, if you're crazy enough! I'm going back to St. Louis on the nine-o'clock train!"

There was a chorus of agreement. But the little runt in the glasses said, "I'll give it a shot. You say you're providing me an armed escort?"

"Yep. You can ride with No-Nose and Widowmaking Wilson. What's your name, by the way?"

"I'm Stanley Cabot, from Boston Mass."

"Well, put her there, Big Stan. Anybody else got the sand in his craw to do the job he come all this way to do?"

Another, bigger man said, "Oh, hell; I signed on because I'd never had any adventures, growing up in Baltimore. I'm Bill Warrington."

"Pleased to know you, Baltimore Bill. You'll be riding with Hellfire Hank and Lonesome Jones. If they hoo-rah you, remind 'em Doc Holliday hailed from Baltimore too."

So, in the end, six of them stayed to do the job and two held out for the nine-o'clock train. Longarm knew he could take down questions with a pencil, and Walleyed McQueen said he'd finished high school. A couple of the other ragged-looking bastards confessed shyly to some book-learning, if Longarm promised to keep it quiet. So by the time they fanned out on their horses, there were ten instead of eight census teams, and if anybody out there didn't aim to answer the questions politely, they'd best start running like hell.

Longarm couldn't be everywhere at once, of course, so he was anxious as well as bored silly as the day wore on. He rode with Calamity Jane and Blackie Slade. They knew all sorts of places where there was a side draw with a squatter's cabin hidden in it, and hoping to stay that way. But as Longarm suspected, none of the folks they questioned saw fit to fire more than surly looks at three folks who looked as mean as anyone in their own families. He filled out form after form, surprised at some of the answers. One man and his teenaged daughter didn't know that the way they were living on a mining claim was frowned on by the law as well as any church Longarm could think of. He put them down as man and wife to account for the three kids they had, then told the moronic miner not to tell anybody anymore that his woman wasn't just a young gal he'd rescued from Indians or something.

Other folks had other things to hide. But, true to his promises, Longarm didn't arrest anybody, although a less ethical lawman could have made himself look pretty good, recovering all that stolen property. The boring part was that nobody he questioned seemed guilty enough of anything to conspire with a whole gang against the federal government. As he asked about outhouses and such, he looked for leads on the missing census takers. Some of the folks remembered one coming by a spell back, but denied gunning any and couldn't say which way they went afterwards.

By late afternoon, Blackie Slade was starting to enjoy playing detective. They were riding through a stretch of second-growth aspen when Blackie pointed off the trail and said, "Look yonder, Longarm. If you're so good, tell me what I see."

Longarm reined in and stared soberly at the aspen tree Blackie meant. Aspen trees didn't turn yellow until late fall, generally. He nodded and said, "You're right. That tree's dead on its roots, and not too far off the trail."

The three of them dismounted. Longarm led the way to the tall skinny aspen and took the smooth olive-green trunk in hand, saying, "Help me pull her out of the earth, Blackie."

So Blackie took hold, and between them they plucked the sapling out by its roots and let its dead and yellowed crown fall aside.

Calamity Jane sniffed and said with a grimace, "Lord of mercy, that sure smells bad."

Blackie Slade stared down at the damp forest loam in the shallow crater and said, "Yep, somebody pulled up that tree, buried something or somebody here, and planted the tree back atop it to slicker us."

Longarm said, "It's somebody, right enough. I was at Shiloh. You never forget the smell."

Calamity Jane said, "Do we have to dig him up, honey bun? He's been in the ground a spell."

Longarm shook his head. "He can stay there for now. Nobody else from Deadwood is missing, and the three bodies missing from the stagecoach ambush wouldn't smell so bad this early. So we know it's one census taker or another. Who lives close enough to have heard something, Blackie?"

"Nobody," Slade said. "As I read this sign, they laid for the cuss here in this lonesome stretch, then bushwhacked and buried him. The others must have been done much the same way."

Longarm stared up at the sun and said, "I suspicion you're right. It's getting late. We'd best ride back to Deadwood, tell the law about this latest find, and let them send a buckboard and some quicklime out for it."

They rode back with their day's work to find that all the

other teams had made it too. Little bespectacled Stanley had collected the most data, but they'd all done a fair job and they all said things had gone more smoothly than they'd expected. Longarm told them to knock off for the day and headed for his own hired room, feeling a mite tuckered for some reason.

But a tall, tight-lipped man in a neat, sober-looking suit was waiting for him in the lobby under an artificial palm that looked more natural than he did. He introduced himself as a special investigator from the Census Bureau, and said his name was Calvin Worth, but that Longarm could call him Cal.

That hardly seemed possible, but they seemed to be hitting it off until Longarm told him what he'd just done. Worth scowled and said, "That's most irregular, sir. You're not from the Census Bureau. You had no right to take command like that. You're not as qualified as Howard Redfern."

"You're wrong, Cal. Calamity Jane is more qualified than he is, right now, since she's still alive. I'll allow we might have failed to dot a few *i*'s and to cross some *t*'s. But some information is better than none. You can take over in the morning if you like, provided your outfit pays the hired guns. I never come to ask folks how many holes they had in their outhouses. Speaking of which, how's the census coming in other parts?"

Worth shrugged and said, "It's been finished almost everywhere but here. We haven't even had trouble in other parts of the Dakotas, as a matter of fact. At the moment, the official population stands at a little over ninety thousand. We'd have a clearer picture if we had the results of the Deadwood census. The Homestake people were good enough to fill in mailed questionnaires for the men they have working in Lead."

"You trust those figures?"

"Of course. Why shouldn't we? Why would they lie?"

Longarm frowned and said, "Don't know. It's easy enough to double-check with the union. I doubt the Knights Of Labor voted all that much for Senator Hearst. But we still got us a problem. At least two of your census takers were last seen alive headed down that way."

"My God, do you think they were murdered in the town of Lead?"

"Not *in* the town. More likely on the trail. I've spoke to folks along the short ride, and I'll be disappointed in my trusting nature if any I know of done the deeds. But I mean to have another look at the summer leaves down Homestake way."

Calvin Worth shook his head and said, "I still can't see any *motive,* can you?"

"No, damn it. I've spent a lot of the taxpayers' money looking into the doings of the Homestake syndicate, and they come up smelling like roses, no matter who I ask. The price of gold ain't fluctuating spooky on the market; they ain't having union trouble; nobody's been trying to buy or sell big blocks of gold-mining stock either in Lead or here in Deadwood. The bigger outfits have been trying to gobble up the smaller claims in the neighborhood, but that's just human nature, and Homestake's been winning the old-fashioned way, by just having more money. With the bonanza gold washed out of the easy tailings, the smaller mine outfits are *anxious* to sell out, as a matter of fact. Anyone except a few old hermits can see that the future in these parts belongs to big, expensively geared outfits that can glean the low-grade at a modest but steady profit. Old hermits have been known to shoot a suspected claim-jumper on occasion, but the gang behind this local skullduggery ain't no old hermit. It's a well-financed criminal organization."

"Which takes us back to the motive."

"I know. Ain't it fun to run in circles, Cal? What can you tell me about the similar business out in the California gold fields?"

154

Worth frowned and said, "I didn't know there was one."

"Yeah, I reckon Washington put enough on your plate with the Dakota case. The one in California ain't my business, either. But it's sort of interesting that two teams of census takers are having the same trouble in the vicinity of gold mines. I'd best horn in with a few wires to the marshal out that way."

He asked the man from Washington to settle on whether he wanted to take over as boss of the census crews now. Worth thought and said, "I think I'd better leave well enough alone. I, like you, was sent to get to the bottom of the plot, not to count noses. If we each go our own way, turning over rocks and comparing notes, we double our odds on solving the case, right?"

"There you go, Cal. I got to wash up for supper and try to catch forty winks before the town comes to life again this evening. So if you don't want to take a bath with me, I'll talk to you some more about it later."

They parted, and Longarm went upstairs to bathe and change. By the time he was clean enough to matter, he was too tired to face the awful vittles they served at this hotel. So he flopped naked across the bed and decided he'd eat something sensible, like chili con carne, later that night. They hadn't changed the linen, and the bed smelled of Penny. He fell asleep feeling wistful about that.

Chapter 12

It was dark out when Longarm woke to the sound of gunfire and moved over to the window, naked. But the gunplay was just a drunk, mad at a lamppost for some reason, so he started to go back to bed, but then decided he might as well get up. It was just as well that he did. He was just buckling on his gun rig when there came a knock on the door. He peered out, saw two gents standing there politely, and opened up. They said they were territorial law sent by Pierre. While he poured hotel tumblers of Maryland rye all around, they went on to ask him what the hell was going on; whatever it was, it was making the territorial government nervous as anything.

He filled them in; it was tedious how folks kept asking the same fool questions about the case that Longarm couldn't answer. He said, "I'm going down to send some wires while I see if there are any replies to some earlier ones I sent all over creation. After that, I mean to arrest the sheriff. You boys are welcome to come along if you like."

The senior of the two men said, "We wouldn't miss it for the world. I know a fed can arrest a local lawman, but ain't you supposed to have some sort of charge?"

Longarm said, "Sure. I'm nailing him on criminal malfeasance. He covered up first-degree murder by failing to arrest the murderer and withholding evidence from the local coroner, most likely for profit."

"That sure sounds like Mahoney. But nobody's ever been able to get anything on him before. Do you have any evidence, since you say he's hid it?"

Longarm said, "Not handy, but I know where to reach for it when the time comes. I got to go to the Western Union first. Mahoney's just a side issue."

They trailed him in wonder as he went downstairs and over to the Western Union, then waited politely until he'd read a couple of wires and sent some as well. Then the junior member of the team asked, "Is this sheriff here in cahoots with the gents who've been smoking up the census takers?"

"Not all," Longarm said. "Just one. Let's wait till I arrest him before we jaw about it, boys. It gets tedious repeating the same tale, and no doubt the sheriff will want to hear why he's being arrested, too."

He led them down the street to the sheriff's office. As they arrived, Sheriff Mahoney was just locking up for the night. He put the key in his pocket and said, "Howdy, Longarm. I'm glad I run into you."

Longarm said, "No you ain't. You're under arrest, Mahoney. These boys are the law from Pierre, by the way, in case you were wondering which side they're on."

Mahoney blinked and said, "Thunderation! You can't arrest me. I'm the damned sheriff!"

Longarm said, "Sure I can. You ought to read the Constitution before you violate hell out of it. A federal lawman outranks a county one, even when he's elected decent."

Mahoney looked relieved and asked, "Is that what this is all about? I told you it was the other party voted them dead folks. Do I look dumb enough to ask Wild Bill to vote for my election?"

"No, but you was mighty dumb to cover up for that Avenging Angel last night. His private license had no standing here in Dakota, and even if it had, he gunned down a man who wasn't wanted anywhere, even by his wife. How much did he promise you of the bounty money, the usual finder's fee?"

Mahoney went for his gun with a snarl.

Longarm had been hoping he would, for trials were tedious as hell.

So, as Mahoney fell dead at Longarm's feet with a .44 round in his lung and another in his heart for good measure, Longarm shook his head and said, *"That* was sure dumb."

The senior territorial lawman gasped, "That's no argument! Where in hell did they teach you to cross-draw like that, Longarm?"

"I dry-fire at myself in the mirror. As I was saying when this old boy got silly, a leftover Avenging Angel trailed a runaway Mormon couple to these parts. He had no call to arrest or gun anyone. He was told polite by me and other lawmen to back off. But he was a zealot and paid us no mind. The kids he was after are long gone, but he didn't know that. He didn't know the folks he was hunting by sight. The fanatics who sent him after them must have imported him from another old-fashioned neck of the desert. He went about asking if anyone had seen a blonde gal and a dark man arriving recent. Howard Redfern and his wife, Penny, wasn't Mormons and didn't look at all like the kids he was after, but they was recent arrivals and had the right hair. So he stalked and gunned Redfern, aiming to kidnap the blonde later. The way I put it together, without this dead rascal here to fill in the blanks, is that after the shooting, Brother William approached Sheriff Mahoney to help him get the dead man back to Nevada, where he thought they was willing to *pay* for it! Mahoney neither knowed nor gave a damn who he'd killed, once they'd settled on a figure. So the late Howard Redfern is on his way to a bitty town in Nevada. Once he gets there, the Nevada law is going to be interested as hell to see who claims the body. The railroad was good enough to give me the destination, and I already notified Nevada to expect it. Anyhow, as you can see, Sheriff Mahoney was party to the murder of an innocent bystander, withheld criminal evidence, and just tried to draw on a federal officer. That ought to hold the son of a bitch."

The senior territorial said, "Pierre will be forever grateful. But how does this tie into the missing census takers?"

"It don't. Like I said, it was a side issue. That's the trouble with crooks. They go on acting crooked and refuse to stand aside when I'm on another case entire. You boys have no idea how many wrong trees I've wound up barking under that way in my time."

"You're wrong. We're lawmen too. What do you figure we ought to do with this dead sheriff, send him to Nevada?"

"Oh, I'll see if the coroner's about and—oh, never mind, here comes the town law."

The local lawman came legging it up the street, responding to the sound of gunplay. As he saw Mahoney lying there, he gasped, "Great balls of fire! Who gunned the sheriff?"

So Longarm had to explain all over again, and by the time he sat down to his chili con carne, he was hungry as a bitch wolf and it was almost time to go back to bed.

His sheets were still haunted by the musky scent of Penny's passion, but he was too tired to fret about sleeping alone. He didn't want to make a habit of it, but he found it a restful novelty.

The next few days were pure hell. Not because anything happened, but because it didn't. As the census went on smoothly, Longarm felt like a sentry on guard at a dull post.

He couldn't relax his guard, because he never knew when something would happen. But it got boring as hell, just waiting. By this time, word had spread about the pistol-whipping that No-Nose Nolan had given a recluse who tried to refuse to answer polite questions, so nobody else made much of a fuss as the handful of dudes and the posse of hardcases tore all over, taking names and asking questions. It was starting to look as though the other side had given up. But why? As Longarm and Cal Worth went over the questionnaires at the hotel, they searched in vain for something worth hiding that seriously. They couldn't find a damned thing. Folks in the Deadwood area tended to be rough-hewn, but nobody had anything more serious to hide than a little incest, child molesting, or a few head of stock they might not have a bill of sale for.

Meanwhile, they found four of the missing men in an advanced state of decomposition. So they could assume the others had wound up under an aspen or down some abandoned try-hole that nobody had a record on at the claims office.

The same claims office said business was slow, and nobody seemed to be striking new color anywhere about. Cal Worth suggested that somebody might have hit a rich placer he was working on his own, and didn't want to be pestered by tax collectors and such. Longarm didn't think so.

He explained, "Back in '76, everybody west of the Muddy who owned a pick or shovel tore through these hills in the wake of the vamoosing Lakota. If there was a pocket of high-grade within a hundred miles, somebody would have tripped over it in the rush. Besides, it would cost less to file a proper claim and pay the modest taxes than it would to hire a gang of gunhands."

He reached into his inside coat pocket thoughtfully, took a wire out to read it over, and said, "Funny thing, though. I haven't been able to identify any of the rascals I gunned along the way. But the Colorado State Prison tells me they just paroled a mess of long-termers for good behavior."

"Colorado? This is Dakota, and as I remember, the Colorado census was finished on time, with no problems."

"Yeah. It makes one wonder, don't it? The Jezebel that the gang saddled me with joined up with me in Denver, too."

Worth shrugged and said, "Well, obviously the gang has connections all over, since they're pulling the same thing in the California gold fields."

"No they ain't," Longarm said. "They've stopped out in the Mother Lode, just like here. The Sacramento marshal's office wired me that they found two of the missing census takers down an old mineshaft near El Dorado. But meanwhile, the second crew's finished up and, like us, the census they turned in ain't even interesting. The folks living in the area are just the sort of folks you'd expect to find around a gold camp. Ain't that a bitch?"

"It's a pure wonder, too! They *had* to be hiding *something!* Maybe the idea was to cover up just long enough to move somebody or something in or out."

"I thought of that. Asked the locals lots of questions about it, too. Nobody around Deadwood remembers seeing dray wagons or even strange riders in serious numbers. The local law would know if anything worth stealing was missing. But, save for the killing of the census takers, it's been fairly peaceable in these parts, considering."

"Let's go over the gold prices again, then."

"I sure wish you wouldn't, Cal. I've been reading stock-market reports until I'm getting cockeyed. Gold ain't going either way enough to kill for. Silver's acting up. There's all this talk about bimetalism back East, so silver is going up and down like a kid jerking off. But they don't mine silver here or in the Mother Lode, so let's not waste time on it. I don't know about you, but it's nigh suppertime and I'm hungry enough to eat the grub they serve here. You coming?"

Worth said he wanted to study the reports some more, so Longarm left him and made his way to the dining room, where he found that the others had already just about cleaned up all the rolls.

He sat down next to a sallow-looking jasper and said, "Evening, Collins. How'd she go today?"

The census taker said, "I'm about done. By the way, that's Collins over there across the table. I'm Burkett."

Longarm said, "Sorry. It's hard keeping the faces and names straight after you've been asking names all day. You say you've about finished your sweep?"

"Yes, thank God. I rode with Calamity Jane this afternoon. Is she serious about wanting to do it up against a tree, standing on her head?"

"Don't know. I suspicion she'd do it flying, if she could figure how. If you did it any way at all with her, I'd advise you to see the doc down the street before he closes for the night."

Burkett laughed and said, "I'm afraid I was forced to pass on her kind offer. I have a weak stomach. By the way, she says you and her and Wild Bill Hickok did it all sorts of ways, that time the three of you were snowed in up in the South Pass."

Longarm sighed and said, "I've been snowed in, but never with her, praise God from whom all blessings flow."

Then he stared hard at the empty roll platter in front of him and gasped, "By God, that's it!" and jumped up from the table.

He almost ran over Cal Worth coming in the door. Worth asked him where he was going in such a hurry, and Longarm snapped, "Denver, if I can make the next train. You boys will be all right here now. The rascals we're after ain't here in Dakota. I should be hogtied and whipped for a fool. I should have seen it right off!"

And then he was on his way. He knew it was impolite to run off without explaining further, but he had to get himself and his possibles over to the depot, pronto, and he'd just told Cal Worth the case here didn't matter anymore.

Chapter 13

Longarm didn't meet anybody interesting on the long ride back to Denver, so he was feeling ready for action when he walked into the office at the Federal Building. Marshal Vail looked up from his desk to ask, "Back so soon? All right, suppose you tell me who was plotting agin the government of these United States, and did you arrest them or act your usual surly self?"

Longarm blew smoke out through his nostrils like a frisky stud and said, "The plot wasn't agin the government. Not the whole government, anyways. Only one senator. Poor old George Hearst."

Vail frowned up at him and answered, "You mean the part-owner of that Homestake mine? Nothing's happened in Lead, let alone at the Homestake holdings, damn it!"

"I know. Just like all the stuff that happened near the Hearst mine in California was well off company property.

They were never interested in the infernal census. They were out to distract Senator Hearst."

"Hell, Longarm, the old gent don't live in either California or Dakota. He abides in Washington, D.C. most of the time. Why didn't they send the guns to Washington if they wanted to assassinate Senator Hearst?"

Longarm shook his head and said, "Pay attention, Billy. I said they aimed to *distract* him, not to *murder* him. When congress ain't in session, the senator's at his home in California. Only this year the senator was sitting on a special committee to fix the price of gold and silver bullion. They likely picked him because he was a mining man and would know the subject. But the rascals plotting to make a killing on the futures exchange didn't want a mining expert on that committee. They wanted him *off* it, to swing the votes their way. So they started trouble near both of his main Western holdings, knowing a man gets nervous when his property's threatened. It worked. The senator's on his way West at the moment to find out what in hell is going on around his posted fences. Naturally, when he gets home, he won't find anything. But meanwhile, he can't advise or vote worth mention in Washington, see?"

"Of course I see. I ain't stupid. But it seems like a mess of trouble to go to, just to boost the price of gold a few points. With the economy starting to prick up, the currency situation is stable and gold ain't fluctuating worth mention."

"No, but *silver* is. I don't know all the ins and outs of the bimetalism argument, but I do know silver is being traded like hell, so a man in the know can make a killing, no matter which way silver goes. *If* he knows ahead of the others, that is."

Vail pursed his lips and said, "Thunderation! Colorado is a silver-mining state, too!"

"I figured you'd see the light if you'd open your ears and listen, Billy. Colorado State Prison reports a rash of sudden releases, too, which means the politicos who pulled those particular strings are likely high up the local totem pole. The prison board was sort of coy about just how come all those long-termers reformed all at once, but they did give me some names and records. They were all gunhands who'd do anything to get out. Some of them were sent to mess up the census both places, near the senator's holdings, to draw his attention from business in Washington. Some others were sent to head me off, in the event I got to Deadwood alive."

Vail laughed and said, "I see they were right. But now what do we do? The slickers have won. The senator's left Washington like they wanted, and all the folks who could have led us back to their doorstep seem to be dead or vanished into thin air."

Longarm took a drag of smoke and said, "Not all of 'em, Billy. You remember that gal in the egret hat that you saddled me with?"

"Yeah, I read your night letter about them gunning her to shut her up. Since even her body is buried in some unmarked grave at the moment, I fail to see how she can testify worth mention, old son."

"Charity can't, but the man who introduced you to her *can*. I owe you an apology, Billy. I put it down as trusting foolishness on your part when I first discovered we'd been hoodwinked. But you're a smart old buzzard. So now all we have to do is arrest the gent who introduced you to her, see?"

Vail looked embarrassed as he said, "I checked with the Census Bureau to double-check you, and you were right. Nobody named Doyle ever worked for their Denver office, Longarm. I reckon I was asleep at the switch when the rascal came in like he owned the place and asked me to have you escort her up to Deadwood."

Longarm shook his head firmly and said, "I don't believe you're that dumb, no offense. You *knew* the man, Billy. That was the slick part. You knew his face, but you didn't

165

have any particular name connected up to it. He was just a face you remembered meeting up with in official circles. It came to me in Deadwood, when I called one of the gents I'd been working with for days by the wrong handle. We all do that sometimes. Think back on the two of them coming in here to your office, and tell me true if you'd have bought the story off a man you'd never seen before!"

Vail nodded thoughtfully and said, "By gum, you're right! I *had* seen the jasper somewhere before, and when he said his name Doyle and asked if I remembered him, I nodded like a goddamn fool and said I did! Him and that treacherous she-male must have laughed fit to bust behind my back!"

"No they didn't, Billy. They knew human nature too well to laugh at you for being only human-natured."

But Vail wasn't listening. He was thinking. Hard. He said, "He don't work for the Census Bureau. When you told me I'd been fooled, I took a mighty hard look at everyone over there. He don't work here in the Federal Building, either. I ain't that stupid. Thunderation! Where in hell *did* I see that rascal afore? I know I ain't seen him lately, for I've been looking for the son of a bitch on my own time."

Longarm went over to the filing cabinet and took out some folders as he said, "I figured he couldn't be a fellow federal employee. On the other hand, you wouldn't have trusted him, had you not seen him more than once."

"That's for damned sure. What are you looking for, Longarm?"

"Lawyers," Longarm replied, explaining, "The only member of the general public that a federal marshal's likely to see often enough to know on sight would be a lawyer who appears in the courtrooms down the hall. Me and the other deputies get to stand in there, bored out of our minds, whilst we guard federal prisoners. But you fat cats run into them in the hall a lot, right?"

"I follow your drift," Vail said. "But damn it, Longarm,

have you any notion how many members of the Colorado bar there are?"

"Sure. At one time or another I've sat there listening to every one of the bastards drone on in pig latin by the hour. We can start by eliminating the regulars, and we can skip one-shot gents who've only been here for a short hearing. The face had to nod at you a few times, but not often enough for you to wonder who it was, see?"

He took out a pencil stub and started writing names as he added, "You'd best get Henry to hire us a cab, boss, unless you aim to walk all over Denver with me."

Vail nodded and got up to see to it as Longarm found the name of a lawyer for a silver-mining outfit, who had appeared last month for a single but protracted case.

By the time Vail came back, Longarm had a list of thirteen names. As they headed out, Longarm handed his boss the list, and Marshal Vail said thirteen was an unlucky number. Longarm said, "I know. It'll be unlucky as hell for at least one of those lawyers if your eagle eye recalls his face. I would have put more names down, Billy, but there wasn't all that many who was qualified to be suspects."

Vail scanned the list as they went down the hall, and on the marble stairs he said, "I got it down to seven, now. I happen to know half a dozen of these lawyers better than you do. I like the number seven better too. But it's still going to take us all day to hunt all seven down."

"Now you know how I feel about some of the jobs you send me on. How about that one called Fletcher? He was the one I aimed to look up first."

Vail nodded and said, "I would have too, in your place. I know he pesters folks for the silver lobby. Unfortunately, I know the ugly bastard on sight. He's only been in federal court on one recent occasion, as you noticed, but I've met him more than once, up at the State House. He's the personal lawyer of State Senator Lyme."

Longarm digested that as they went out and climbed in

the hired cab out front. Then, as they settled back, he told the driver to head for the State House. As they pulled away, he told Vail, "Leadville Larry Lyme ain't just a state senator. He deals in silver futures. Some say he wheels as well as deals. Started out grubstaking prospectors back in the sixties and wound up a silver tycoon with a brownstone house on Sherman Avenue and a senior seat in the State House."

Vail snorted, "Don't lecture me on the history of Colorado, son. I was here when it was being made. I was a deputy like you when I investigated claims that some of Leadville Larry's mining ventures had had lethal effects on his original partners, too. That's how come I know him and his lawyers so well. I'd enjoy putting that old scoundrel in the box almost as much as I'd like being alone in a hotel room with Lillian Russell. But we're wasting time. The gent who introduced them egret feathers ain't Fletcher or any other lawyer on the senator's payroll."

"I'll buy that, Billy," Longarm said. "The man calling himself Doyle could have been a business associate or something. A man meets all sorts of folks, wheeling and dealing in silver futures."

"Then what in thunder are we headed for the State House for? They don't deal in silver futures at the state legislature."

As the cab swung uphill on Colfax, Longarm said, "They are today. It was in the *Post*. They're holding hearings on how this bimetalism bull is supposed to work. There's a lot of money riding on how Washington and the mining states peg the ratio of gold and silver bullion. So wouldn't you be in the gallery if you was in the silver business, Billy?"

Vail started to shake his head. Then he shrugged and said, "Well, it beats tearing all over town in this cab. But I still think it's a wild shot. Seems to me it would be playing a mite risky to send a regular from the State House over to con me. I visit them marble halls fairly regular."

"I know. And they know you're generally holding down that chair in your office at this time of day too, no offense.

They had to take a chance and send you a State House regular, Billy. We've agreed you'd have been a pest about identification and such if you hadn't recognized the rascal on sight when he brought Charity Kirby to see you. Someone lurking regular about the State House works even better than a face familiar in the halls at the Federal Building. You started out recognizing him as someone or other you'd run into in some other government surroundings."

The cab pulled up to the side entrance at Colfax and Sherman. They got out and told the cabbie to wait, just in case. Then Longarm gazed up at the golden dome looming high above them in the sunlight and said, "My, that's pretty. You ever go up in the dome, Billy? You can see Pike's Peak from there on a clear day."

Vail snorted and asked, "Do I look like a tourist? The senate chambers is on the main floor and the public viewing gallery is upstairs. Which level do you fancy?"

Longarm pointed his chin at a flight of stone steps and said, "Birdseye view, for openers. From the gallery we can see everyone on the floor, as well as any and all interested bystanders."

So they walked along the marble corridor to where a uniformed guard stood in front of an imposing set of closed doors with the words *Public Gallery* posted above them. Vail reached for the handle, and the guard looked awkward and said, "You can't go in there today, gents. It's a closed session. The public ain't invited."

Vail took out his ID and said, "We ain't the public, we're the law. So open up."

The guard hesitated, then nodded and produced a key ring to let them into the gallery as Billy Vail scowled hard at him. Inside, they found themselves alone on a balcony overlooking the action below. A florid-faced fat man had the floor and was yelling a lot about "free silver," while the other politicos down there tried to stay awake. Vail stood by Longarm at the rail of the gallery and muttered, "That's

169

Leadville Larry over there, sitting under all the silver hair, reading the newspapers."

"I know who Senator Lyme is, damn it. Take a gander at the other rascals down there on the floor. Forget the big shots and peruse the clerks and pages and such for a face you know well enough to remember but not to place."

"I'm looking, damn it!" Vail said. "It ain't one of them young pages. The gent who said he was with the Census Bureau was somewhere between you and me in age. He had on a gray tweed suit and a flashy stickpin, now that I study on it."

"Forget his duds and just think of the face. A man can change his clothes. Picture everyone down ther in that same gray suit instead of what he might be wearing today."

Vail did so. Then he gasped, turned, pointed at the closed doors behind them, and said, "Goddamn! It was him! That hall guard!"

Longarm didn't wait to congratulate his boss on his memory. He was headed for the door as he drew his Colt. As he opened it and ran out in the hall, he saw the dark-uniformed guard making tracks down the marble floor toward the rotunda. He'd obviously had his ear to the door panels and had't liked what he'd heard Billy Vail shout.

Longarm shouted, "Give it up, friend. The State House is surrounded!"

The bluff didn't stop the running guard, but it must have worked some, because instead of running down the stairs when he came to the circular open space under the capitol dome, he ran *up* them. When Longarm reached the next level, the man was nowhere to be seen.

But Longarm had a restless nature and the catlike curiosity of the self-educated. As he'd told Vail, he'd explored the Capitol in the past, wanting to know what Pike's Peak looked like from Denver. So he moved over to a nondescript door and opened it, revealing a spiral staircase of stamped-steel steps. He cocked his head and listened; though the fugitive was trying to move softly, the grit on the soles of his shoes betrayed his footsteps as he circled above. Longarm nodded to himself and started up the spiral staircase. They ended at another doorway on a higher level. Longarm took a deep breath, crouched low, and burst out on the circular balcony running around the interior of the dome.

The armed guard hadn't gone outside to use the penny telescopes on the observation platform. He'd circled to the far side. As Longarm crabbed sideways coming out the doorway, the fugitive fired across the gulf, splintering marble chips off the stone balustrade close enough to make Longarm duck his head below the waist-high stone rail. Longarm knew he could crawl around the bulletproof balustrade to the far side, but if he tried that, the other would just complete the circle and be back to the spiral stairs by the time Longarm reached his present position. If he stayed here, covering the doorway to the only way out, it was a Mexican standoff until Billy Vail caught up. Where the hell was the marshal, and—more important—would Billy have sense enough to come out that bitty doorway low and sudden?

Longarm decided he'd best not wait. He moved along the safe side of the stone rail until he could just see the doorway as well as give the impression that he was circling. Then he shouted. His words echoed hollowly under the big dome as he suggested, "If you'll turn state's evidence, I can likely fix you up with a short sentence, pard. I know it's tedious making little rocks out of big ones, but it sure beats hanging."

No answer. But he heard the scrape of leather on stone. If the echo hadn't tricked him, the invisible other had moved counter-clockwise a few yards to maintain their positions on opposing sides of the big circle.

Longarm called out, "Look, you know you ain't fixing to get out of here standing tall unless you surrender sensible. The only charge we have on you is impersonating a federal official. The folks you work for have killed all sorts of people. They killed that girl you introduced to my boss. They shot her to shut her up when they suspected I was getting onto her. Are you dumb enough to hang loyal to folks like that? What's ailing you? Cat got your tongue?"

It didn't work. The man was either dumb as hell or deeper in the plot than he wanted to discuss with a federal lawman. Longarm reached in his coat pocket with his free hand and took out a fistful of loose .44-40 rounds. He tossed one small but heavy cartridge, and when it had finished clattering on the marble, he tossed a second, farther, to make it sound like he was a full quarter-turn of the dome from where he really crouched. The guard must have thought he was coming around fast and reckless, for he panicked and made his own noisy run for it, crouched low. As he came in view, circling to get back to the spiral stairs, Longarm threw down on him and snapped, "Freeze!"

But the wide-eyed rascal wouldn't. He spotted Longarm crouched there, covering him, and raised the pistol in his hand to return the favor. So Longarm fired, and the dome echoed awesomely to the roar of his double-action .44 as the guard straightened up, dropped his own gun with a clatter of steel on stone, and clutched at his chest to stagger back and sideways until his hip hit the rail and he went over, screaming.

Longarm rose and looked over the rail. He gazed down on the figure far below him, spread on the marble like a stepped-on cockroach. Other figures appeared down there, looking just as small but in better shape, and on their feet. Billy Vail called up, "Can't you ever do anything quietly, Longarm? I wanted to talk to this rascal, but now look at him. He's flatter than a cake that fell in the oven!"

Longarm called down, "I already talked to him, Marshal Vail. Is Senator Lyme handy down there?"

The tiny Vail pointed at a tiny figure with silver hair and shouted up, "Right here. We was just discussing your boisterous ways. Why?"

"You'd better put the cuffs on him, then. I can't reach him from up here. His gunslinging crony told me who he worked for, before he made a last-minute break for it. I thought we was having some friendly plea-bargaining, but I reckon he changed his mind. I'll come down and fill you all in."

He moved over to the dead man's gun on the floor and picked it up to pocket it. Who was to say, now, where it had been when the rascal went over the rail?

By the time he got down to the floor of the rotunda, Billy Vail had Leadville Larry Lyme with his hands cuffed in front of him. The senator was yelling that nobody could arrest such an important personage, while the other State House folks pretended they didn't know him anymore. Longarm nodded to him and said, "Howdy, Senator. Your Mr. Doyle, laying over yonder, must have been fond of Charity Kirby, whoever she was. You boys made a mistake in gunning her. He agreed he didn't owe no loyalty to a boss who used little folks to wipe his ass. But then, as you see, he made a break for it."

Leadville Larry sneered and said, "You're full of shit and he's full of lead, and squashed flat besides. His confession won't stand up in court and you know it."

"Let's take him out the side entrance, Marshal Vail. Cab's still waiting, and as you see, he's going to jaw at us all the way to the federal lockup. So we'd best get it over with."

As they loaded him in the cab, the red-faced and silver-haired prisoner snapped, "I'll have you both transferred to Alaska for this! I don't care what Malone told you. It's my word against yours now, and I'm a very powerful man in this state."

Longarm made a mental note of the name and said, "Not anymore. Now that we have the full story, it won't take much to build our case agin you. Five will get you ten it turns out your influence got Malone his job here at the State House, despite his record. The folks at the State Prison will likely remember who twisted their arms to get those gun-slingers of yours out early. And when U.S. Senator Hearst hears why you caused him all that worry, *he'll* likely use some influence too. If I was you, I'd try to cut my losses, so why don't you? We know you was here in Denver, fiddling with the price of silver, while your hired guns were murdering folks in California and the Dakotas. What do you think, Billy? Can we let him off with murder two if he makes a clean breast of it?"

On the other side of the prisoner, Vail shook his head and said, "I don't want him to cooperate. I've been wanting to see him hang too long. It's murder one when you kill someone, whether you finger's on the trigger or not."

Longarm could have kicked him. But the prisoner's face was ashen as he sort of cowered down in his seat and said, "Listen, I swear I never said to kill anybody. The boys were only supposed to stir things up around Senator Hearst's holdings. Any killing they did was on their own."

By the time they'd transported him to the federal lockup, Longarm was grinning like a kid turned loose in a candy shop. Leadville Larry, in his attempt to wriggle out of the hangman's noose, had incriminated himself beyond repair. As they left him to contemplate the walls of his cell until a federal grand jury could get around to him, Longarm laughed and said, "That went better than a lot of poker games I've played. We make a good team, Billy."

Vail shrugged. "Hell, it wasn't all that hard, seeing as the guard confessed before you spread him on the floor like a rug back there."

Then Vail shot Longarm a sharp look and added, "You *did* say he talked before he went over the rail, didn't you, old son?"

Longarm said, "Ask me no questions and I'll tell you no lies, boss."

"Jesus H. Christ! You pulled a poker bluff! Don't look so infernally innocent at me, Longarm! I know you of old.

174

But every time I think I know what balls you have, you produce some more! You let me arrest a state senator without a goddamn single shred of evidence!"

"Now don't get your bowels in an uproar, Billy. It worked, didn't it?"

"It wouldn't have, if he hadn't been guilty! We ain't supposed to arrest folks on educated guesses, damn it! There was a whole mess of big shots there you could have accused so wild, Longarm. What if you'd guessed wrong?"

"We'd have been in trouble. But they'd have settled for you firing me, since it was me and not you who made the charge. I had to chance it, Billy. Like you suspicioned, I only had a process of elimination to go on. But he eliminated better than anyone else, and it had to be one damned politician or another who pulled all those strings."

Vail whistled softly. "You sure don't take your job too serious."

"I take it more serious than you think," Longarm replied. "That silver-headed son of a bitch had a mess of innocent folk swatted like flies for a piss-poor reason. It ain't *right* to let bastards like him run about off a leash! What's a job, when you consider how many times I've risked my whole ass going down a dark alley to arrest a crook who only came to Leadville Larry's knee?"

"Well, your wild call worked, and as long as we're pulling a poker bluff, I mean to get a list of names from the warden at the state prison. You do recall how the senator implicated him a mite in the cab just now, don't you, old son?"

"I surely do, boss. Any that ain't picked up in the first dragnet don't figure to run loose too long. They was dumb enough to get arrested the first time, and now that they won't have leadership, money, or influence, they won't last long on the owlhoot trail."

"Yeah, where in thunder is that cab I told to wait out here?"

"He didn't wait, as anyone can see, Billy. But the office ain't that far. It's getting sort of late, though. Could I have the rest of the afternoon off?"

"I reckon you've earned it," Vail said. "But where are you in such an itch to get to, Longarm?"

"Oh, thought I'd drift out to the orphanage this afternoon."

"You worried about that young gal you saved from a life of sin?"

"Ain't sure I did. They have to let her out in a couple of years. But it might be interesting discussing her probable future with a certain matron out there. I missed the party she invited me to the other day. The least I can do is tell her about another shindig they're having at the Grange hall this evening."

Vail chuckled and said, "Good hunting, then. But make sure you get to the office on time, come morning."

"Grange dance will be over well this side of midnight, Billy," Longarm replied innocently.

"That's what I mean. I know you when you get a late-night start at a female. If you had any sense, you'd wait for the weekend to start up with a new conquest, you horny rascal."

Longarm grinned crookedly and said, "If I had any sense, I wouldn't even talk to the infernal orphan herder. Pretty as she may be, I face an uphill climb on a slippery slope. I doubt she'll conquest worth mention."

Vail looked puzzled and asked, "Why in hell are you bothering with her, then? There's more she-folk in and about Denver than a man can shake his dick at, and some are said to be willing as well as lonesome."

Longarm said, "I know. But I've never been able to resist a tough case, and what the hell, I've just about recovered from all the easy stuff I've been getting of late. I'll see you in the morning early, Lord willing and the creeks don't rise."

Vail snorted and said, "I know what's likely to rise betwixt here and morning, and if you ain't there by high noon, I swear I'll fire you!"

Watch for

LONGARM AND THE GREAT TRAIN ROBBERY

forty-sixth novel in the bold
LONGARM series from Jove

coming in July!

A shape detached itself from the shadows beneath the veranda to reveal itself as a huge, hulking man, standing at least as tall as Longarm, but outweighing the Deputy by at least twenty pounds. None of that extra weight looked like fat, either. He was dressed in a suit, complete with a string tie in place down the front of his grimy white shirt. "Hold it, boy!" the man snapped out at the young wrangler, countermanding Jessica's orders. "Just who is staying with us, Miss Jessie?"

"This doesn't concern you, Higgins," Jessica said.

"As foreman of this here outfit, I guess it'll be me who decides what concerns me or not. With all due respect, Miss Jessie." He grinned, his smile yellow-toothed and resembling that of a grizzly just before it cracks open a beehive. He ambled over to Longarm's horse, patting its flanks as he looked the gelding over. "Fine animal. Don't often see a hand with his own mount." He turned to stare at Longarm. "You signing on as a hand, boy?"

"I'm signing on to dig your grave if you call me 'boy' again," Longarm told him. There was the sound of guffaws swiftly choked off. Four more men stepped out from the interior darkness of the veranda to lean against the railing.

Longarm looked them over. They were wearing expensive Stetsons and shiny Justin boots, though the rest of their clothes were broken down and dusty. Their gunbelts were cracked and scuffed, cinched tightly about their waists. Longarm didn't have to examine their weapons to know that they'd be single-action weapons, working hands' weapons—not the kind of guns that man-killers carried. They were a wolf pack following their big bad he-wolf, Higgins. They could be troublesome when drunk, all of them against one man in the dark; but they were nothing but wind when stared down in broad daylight.

Higgins, however, glancing back at them, did not appear sorry to see them. "You son of a bitch," he said to Longarm.

"Easy, boss," one of the men on the veranda warned.

"Shut up, Ray," Higgins glowered back over his shoulder. He looked back at Longarm. "I called you a son of a bitch."

"Now that ain't much better than 'boy,'" Longarm drawled. "Try again, else I'll have to fetch me a shovel."

Higgins flushed red. He whipped off his Stetson to wipe at the sweat dewing his brow. He was bald. His hatband had pressed a red ridge across his ivory pate. "You get your horse," he snarled, "and ride off this spread."

"Whether I stay or go is up to Jessica," Longarm explained. "That's *Miss Jessie* to you," he added.

Higgins unbuttoned his suit jacket.

"Easy, old son," Longarm cautioned. "I can see you're carrying your gun in a shoulder rig. You ought to realize there's damn little chance you can outdraw me."

Higgins, his hand hovering in midair, seemed to think that what Longarm had said was good advice.

"This has gone far enough, Higgins," Jessica fumed. "Now get back to work."

"Your daddy made me foreman, and it's my job to take care of you," Higgins argued.

"Your job is to take care of this spread, period," Jessica said.

"Now don't go getting all riled, Miss Jessie." Higgins winked slyly. "You know I only got your best interests at heart."

More men have their eyes on this filly than Texas has cows, Longarm thought to himself. Plain as day, Higgins saw himself as Jessica's beau, regardless of how Jessica saw it.

"Just get back to work," Jessie said disgustedly.

"First I'll take his gun," Higgins replied, pointing at Longarm. "I'm doing it for you, Miss Jessie. With your daddy being shot dead and all, we can't have no strangers being around you armed."

"Higgins, I'm warning you—" Jessica began, but Higgins waved her aside as he strode down the steps of the veranda. "Hush now, girl. Your daddy would want me to do this." He advanced upon Longarm, his hand outstretched. "Give me your gun, boy. Else you'll have to outshoot me and the four behind me."

Longarm prepared himself for trouble, but just then Ki glided between the deputy and the burly foreman.

"Miss Jessica has given you an order, Higgins," the unarmed man said in his soft voice.

"Get out of my way!"

Ki was now less than a yard away from the foreman. He seemed dwarfed by Higgins's hulking form. "You are not being polite to our guest, Higgins."

"Now that Mr. Starbuck is dead, maybe there's no room for you on this spread," Higgins snarled. "What do you think, boys?" he called over his shoulder.

"Get rid of him, boss," one of the men called.

"Bust his hole," another chortled.

"That tears it." Higgins grinned. "Run along, Chinaman—"

Before he could say another word, Ki struck with a roundhouse kick. His torso bent sideways as his leg came around straight and true, his foot catching Higgins beneath the chin.

The foreman rose about six inches in the air, and then fell, to land hard on his butt. By then, Ki was back in a relaxed, standing position. The whole kick and return had taken less time than a rattlesnake takes to strike.

"I am of Japanese ancestry, not Chinese, Higgins," Ki said, staring down at the foreman. "But you needn't grovel in the dirt. Merely apologize."

Higgins lumbered to his feet. He was swearing and spitting

in rage. He tugged out from beneath his jacket a blue-steel Peacemaker. But before he could even thumb back the hammer on the single-action weapon, Ki moved in fast. He swatted Higgins's gun with the edge of his right hand. The Peacemaker went flying off in the direction of the Texas Panhandle as Higgins yelped in surprise and clasped his wrist.

"Shoot the yellow chink!" Higgins shouted in frustration to his men.

Longarm quickly moved toward the veranda, drawing his Colt as he did so. "Let's all stay out of this, boys. What do you say?"

The four men stared at Longarm's Colt. They noticed that its barrel had been cut down to five inches, and that it lacked a front sight. They looked at the cross-draw rig, and then back at the gun trained rock-steady upon them. "He's a gunslick, we can't do nothing!" one of them said. Gradually they lifted their hands toward the pitched roof of the veranda.

"Then I'll kill you myself, chink. With my bare hands," Higgins huffed, now truly resembling a grizzly. He moved warily around Ki, who stood motionless, not even bothering to turn as Higgins attacked from behind.

As the foreman looped both brawny arms around Ki's neck, the smaller man thrust his elbow into the other's solar plexus. Higgins gasped in pain, his arms going limp, now encompassing nothing but thin air. Ki slammed his elbow into Higgins's ribs, and the foreman staggered like a poleaxed steer. Ki swept Higgins's boots out from under the heavy man, using only his own bare foot, but that foot was like a broom sweeping away litter. Higgins landed on his knees, and then toppled all the way to the ground. He rolled over his back, his breath coming in agonized rasps as he clutched at his chest and side.

Light as a feather, Ki knelt beside him. With one hand he tilted Higgins's chin to expose the foreman's throat. "If I struck here," he said, his finger gently tracing Higgins's Adam's apple, "you would choke to death on your own crushed throat."

"Please..." Higgins gasped, his eyes rolling white. Ki's rigid grip had arced his neck back at an impossible angle. Higgins resembled—in more ways than one—a chicken with its neck stretched across the chopping block.

"Or here," Ki continued, ignoring Higgins's plea. He

touched the foreman's nose. "If I struck here, shards of bone would drive themselves into your pig's brain. Your life would bleed out of your ears into the dust—"

"Ki," Jessica called. "Don't. Let him go."

After a moment, Ki smiled and nodded. "Higgins, am I Chinese?"

"No . . ."

"What am I, Higgins?"

"Japanese . . ." the foreman gurgled, and then moaned.

"Half Japanese," Ki remarked. "But close enough, Higgins, close enough."